THE CHOSEN ONE

The Chosen One

MARY'S STORY

C.A. Simonson

CAS Publications

Contents

Introduction

This is a work of fiction. Details have carefully been mined from scripture, history, and legend.
This is a revised version from the first edition published in episodes on Kindle Vella (2021).

As you read, put yourself in Mary's place. How would you have felt? How would you have responded to the angel's message?

What would you have done?
I trust you enjoy *The Chosen One.*

C.A. Simonson

I

THE BETROTHAL

Mary lay back on the makeshift hay bed finding minor respite between contractions. *If I knew how much this hurt when I agreed to be God's handmaiden, would I have still gone through with it?* Her body tightened into another contraction. She tightly grabbed Joseph's hand and held her breath in pain.

"Breathe, Mary. Short, controlled breaths. Breathe," encouraged Joseph.

The contraction subsided, and Mary gave him a weak smile. "Thank you, Joseph. Stay with me. Please." *Sweet Joseph,* she thought. *What a blessed man God has given to be my helpmate.* Mary's mind wandered as she awaited the birth of the king. *It hasn't even been a year yet, and so much has happened.* She thought back to the days of her betrothal and all the events leading to this moment.

#

"Mary!" Seeing her best friend at the well, Hannah ran toward her. "I just heard! Joseph asked for your hand! You're going to get married! Has he talked to your father yet?"

The young teen blushed a bright pink. "Hannah! Slow down! So many questions!" Mary drew her water from the well. "Yes. Joseph talked to Father. He will follow all the Jewish traditions. He offered my father his services for a year."

"Services?" Hannah lowered her jug over the edge of the well as she spoke. "Isn't he supposed to bring a special mohar for the brideswealth?

Mary pulled her jug from the water. "A mohar, or gift seals the marriage contract. And Joseph offered Father a table or a bench, but Father wanted his services instead."

"What kind of services?"

"He would rather have Joseph help with repairs around the house. So, he said he would help with repairs for a year, as per the custom of the mohar. He's a carpenter in Nazareth, you know."

"I know he's a carpenter, and quite a bit older than you. You've had your eye on Jacob or Seth." Hannah gave her friend a sly look.

"I have not," Mary defended and then sighed. "But you are right; Joseph is a lot older than me. You and I both know Jacob or Seth couldn't support a wife for many years." She rolled her eyes. "They're the same age as we are."

Hannah giggled. "But they *are* cute." She lifted her jug from the well. Setting it on the ground, she lowered the next jug into the well. "But why Joseph?"

"Joseph has an established business. He works well with his hands and will provide for me. Besides that, Mother says his bloodline comes from Kings David and Solomon, and that's important. Father picked well."

"What about you, Mary? Do you want to marry Joseph?"

"Father knows what's best for me, and I must respect that. I don't really have much say about it."

"Well, I'm happy for you," said Hannah as she gave Mary a big hug. "When's the big ceremony? The kiddushin?"

"The marriage contract will be signed in a few months," said Mary. "Joseph wanted to give my family enough time to get ready."

"Will I be invited?"

"Are you my best friend?" Mary smiled and hugged Hannah again. "Of course. You will be one of the witnesses to the signing. Joseph will bring his witness, and, of course, my parents will be there, too. Joseph's parents are no longer living, but some of his family might come."

"And then, you will really be betrothed!"

"...and bound by law," added Mary with a serious note.

The girls started walking down the path toward their homes holding the filled water jugs at their sides. Both were absorbed in their own thoughts. After a few minutes, Hannah had to know.

"Have you spoken to him yet, Mary?"

"Who?"

"Joseph, of course, silly. Your betrothed-to-be. Don't you want to know more about him? Or hear what his voice sounds like? Or how he acts toward you?"

Mary gave her friend a sideways glance. "Again with the questions, Hannah. You know we can't speak to each other until after the wedding. That's Torah law."

"Even at the kiddushin?"

"Even then. All communication must go through Joseph's spokesman for a full year until the marriage feast."

"Oh. Well, that's too bad. I would want to know more about the man I'm about to marry. Well, here's my turn-off. See you tomorrow. Sweet dreams about Joseph."

"See you tomorrow," Mary replied as her thoughts turned toward her future husband. *Mother says he's an honorable man. She says I'll find out about him after the marriage and that I can learn to love him. But will I? Can I?*

For one so young, Mary's thoughts ran deep. Her greatest desire of all was to do her best to please God.

II

THE KIDDUSHIN

The next couple of months were a flurry of activities as Mary's family prepared for the kiddushin – the ceremonial signing of the marriage contract. The sacred ceremony was, in many ways, more important than the actual wedding feast. It was a mutual agreement of betrothal one to another – a promise of faithfulness and fidelity.

As Mary hand-stitched beautiful tiny flowers on her veil, she thought about the upcoming day. She knew her parents could not afford a lot of expenses. They were not wealthy, but they had all they ever needed. There would be no fine silks for her wedding canopy. But Mary didn't care. She would be satisfied – *no,* she corrected her thought, *I will be delighted to stand beneath a canopy of flowers for the chupa.*

A knock came at the door.

"Come," Mary called.

Hannah bounced through with girlish glee. Seeing the veil Mary had in her hand, she carefully picked up a corner of the soft fabric and examined the needlework.

"Oh, Mary! This is beautiful work!"

"I want a pretty veil. Mother is working on my wedding garment."

"You are soooo lucky, Mary!" Hannah exclaimed.

"Not lucky – blessed," Mary corrected. "God has blessed me beyond measure and given me a good man to take care of me. Praise Adonai!"

"Just think," said Hannah with dreaminess in her eyes. "In a little over a year, you might become a mother!"

"Hannah! Such talk!" Mary blushed at the thought.

"Well, it's true, Mary. You and Joseph will finally live together then. I just can't wait to have babies of my own. Can you?"

"Someday…" Mary's words trailed as her thoughts became sober.

"Mary?"

"Yes, Hannah?"

"Have you ever thought about giving birth to the Christ-Child? Someday, some lucky woman will get to be the mother of God's Son. Just think," Hannah said in wonder, "It could be you, …or me…or Susanna. One of us could be the Messiah's mother. I wish it could be me."

"You're such a dreamer, Hannah." Mary laughed. "You need a man to make a baby."

"But for the Messiah, it wouldn't. It would have to be a real miracle. It would have to be …." Hannah scrunched her forehead in deep thought, "…in order to be God's Son."

Mary nodded. "It would be a miracle, indeed. …unlike any other. The Torah says He will come from a virgin. I don't understand how that can be –but it sure wouldn't be luck." Mary laughed at her friend again and shook her head. "The woman who bears the Christ-Child, the Son of God, would have to be highly favored and especially blessed of God. I don't know anyone who fits that bill, my friend – including you or me."

#

The day of Kiddushin finally arrived, phase one of the Jewish wedding: the honored tradition of signing the wedding contract. The courtyard looked festive. The Chupa – the wedding canopy arch under which the couple would sign the contract – was hung with fresh ivy and wildflowers.

Hannah arrived early to help Mary get ready. She would witness the signing along with Joseph's friend Marcus.

Rabbi Abram arrived. He would read the marriage contract out loud before the couple and guests. He took his place behind the Chupa and nodded toward Mary's father to start the procession. The rest of the guests took their seats.

Heli, Mary's father, joined Joseph and locked arms with him. Holding a candle in his other hand, they proceeded toward the rabbi. Once they arrived at the Chupa, it was Mary's turn.

Anna took her daughter by the arm, holding a candle in the other hand. "These candles represent peace and joy for your marriage, Mary," Anna whispered. Together, mother and daughter walked the path, meeting Joseph at the front before Rabbi Abram.

Mary stood beside Joseph, her beautiful, embroidered veil covering her face. She beamed as she viewed the handsome man standing tall and strong. *He might be older, but he's a man of character and wisdom. A man of noble upbringing, I can tell,* Mary thought. *I wish he could see me smile and how happy I am today.*

Rabbi Abram began to read the ketubah in the ancient Aramaic. The couple stood in silent reverence until he finished. Then Joseph spoke.

"I don't own much, Mary. I'm only a simple carpenter. But I promise to take care of you and provide for you. I will put a roof over your head and shelter you and our children to come. I will feed and care for you for the rest of our lives together. Today we seal this covenant. I betroth you unto me forever in all faithfulness, affection, and fidelity."

Mary did not speak during this ceremony. Her presence alone spoke agreement with the ritual and with the contract. She simply bowed her head and listened in compliance and humility as Joseph spoke.

The rabbi announced, "We will now sign this sacred ketubah sealing this agreement of marriage. Marcus. Hannah. Please join us as this couple's witnesses."

Joseph took the quill and signed his name, and gave it to Mary. She signed her name. Her parents cosigned to ensure the agreement. Then

Rabbi Abram took the contract, rolled it up, and ceremoniously handed it to Joseph. Joseph held it up, said a silent prayer to God with his eyes lifted toward heaven, and then passed the contract to Mary. Mary gave Joseph a slight nod, accepted the document, and looked toward heaven with closed eyes. She then gave it to her father until the wedding day a year later. She knew if this contract were lost or stolen, the marriage with Joseph could never be consummated, according to Torah law. Father would keep it in a safely guarded place.

#

Afterward, everyone rejoiced with the couple singing, dancing, and eating Anna's luscious cooking. As the guests left, Marcus approached Mary and introduced himself.

"If you need to get a message to Joseph between now and the wedding feast, you must contact me."

Mary nodded. "How will I find you?"

"I'm in the synagogue each Sabbath if you need me."

"What now, Mary?" Hannah interrupted as she helped clean up.

"I wait – and prepare. I occupy and busy myself with preparations until he comes back to get me," said Mary. "Joseph is going to prepare a place for me. When it's ready, he'll come and take me home. We'll have a huge marriage supper and celebrate. Then, we will consummate our marriage and live happily ever after." Mary let out a huge breath as a slight quiver shook her with anticipation.

"I hope he's good to you, Mary."

"I just hope I can be a good and faithful wife," answered Mary. *And I hope I'm ready.*

---

https://www.chabad.org/library/article_cdo/aid/477335/jewish/The-Betrothal.htm

https://www.chicagojewishnews.com/what-can-jewish-bride-say-wedding/

III

DREAMS & VISIONS

Mary loved springtime in Nazareth. The almond blossoms smelled so sweet. After checking on the flax fields, she strolled farther up the hillside and plopped onto the lush green grass. Her heart beat with gratefulness toward Elohim. She began to worship in song and praise to her loving Heavenly Father. Lifting her arms toward heaven, she closed her eyes and gloried in the warm kiss of the sun upon her face. She opened her eyes as a gentle breeze wrapped her in its wisp. God had been so good to her. A wonderful man was about to come into her life, and she could hardly wait.

Mary's mind wandered as she gazed at the floating clouds above, mesmerized by their beauty and changing features. Her mind had been on God a lot, especially after her talks with Hannah. She had pondered the words of her friend for weeks. She and her girlfriends often talked about becoming the mother of the Christ Child. It was part of their teaching: someday, a virgin would bear the Messiah. Every girl wanted to be 'the chosen one.' What an honor it would be to give birth to royalty and deity!

"The woman who bears the Christ Child would be honored above all women," she recited aloud. "Oh, to have such a miraculous honor...unlike any other."

As her eyes watched the clouds, she imagined God looking down upon her. *Am I worthy, Lord? Are you pleased with me?*

Her soul began to overflow with praise and adoration as she felt God's presence surround her. Suddenly a bright light broke through the clouds. She rubbed her eyes that were temporarily blinded by the brilliance. When she opened them, she was startled to see an enormous Being shrouded in beams of light. She quickly sat up and drew her legs to her chest in fright as fear etched her face. Her skin prickled.

"Do not be afraid, Mary. I bring you greetings from God. You are highly favored among women."

His words felt like liquid silk as they soothed her mind of anxiety and shock. She shielded her eyes from his radiance and inhaled deeply. *What did he mean? Highly favored?*

"Don't fear," he told her again. "The Lord is with you."

Could it be true? Am I dreaming?

"You have found great favor with God. You will conceive and bear a son. You will call his name, Jesus."

This troubled her spirit greatly. She drew back in the unspoken question. *Jesus? Meaning 'he will save' – a Savior?*

The angel continued, "He will be great and shall be called the Son of God. His kingdom shall never end."

Mary's head swirled with conflicting thoughts. *The Messiah? But scripture says the Messiah will come from Bethlehem. I'm from Nazareth – and I'm betrothed to Joseph.* A frown creased her forehead as she decided to be bold before this angelic being. *I will dare to speak.* Taking a deep breath, she stood before him.

"But how?" she asked the angel. "How can these things be? I've not been with any man. I am still a virgin."

"The Holy Spirit will come over you, and the power of the Most High will overshadow you."

Mary marveled at his answer. She didn't think that was how it worked. *Can I trust his words? He said he came from God, and his name was Gabriel. If I choose to believe, will I be willing to be the chosen one?*

The consequences could be enormous. She knew the answer immediately. *Gabriel said I was highly favored and blessed by God. And I trust God to take care of me. I will believe.*

In surrender to her own will, she bowed her head and answered. "I am the Lord's handmaiden. May your words be fulfilled as you have said."

Then as suddenly as he appeared, he disappeared – leaving her with more questions. Mary believed without a doubt that God had chosen her to be the mother of His Son. She opened her heart in worship as she raised her hands and face in praise again. She spoke in a loud voice toward heaven, "God, I am your servant! Let it be as you said!" She closed her eyes and felt the warmth of God's power envelop her in holy love.

She wasn't sure how long she had been on the hillside, but something felt different as she made her way home. She wanted to run tell Hannah her great news, but would she make fun of her? Then a scarier thought entered her mind. What would Joseph say? Would he believe her or leave her? How could she make him believe she carried the Holy One? Would he think she lying or out of her mind? How could she even relay her message without talking to him face to face?

"Mary, where have you been? It's nearly dusk! You've been out all afternoon!" Her mother scolded the teen as she kneaded the dough. "Did you get lost in your daydreams again?"

"Mother," Mary was breathless with excitement and awe. "You'll never believe what just happened to me!"

Glancing at her wide-eyed daughter raised more concern. "Mary! Slow down–and sit down!" Anna said. "Your face is flushed. You're out of breath. What's wrong?"

But telling her mother about the amazing experience only brought more questions of concern.

––––––––––

Luke 1:26-38; Matthew 1:18

IV

——————

IS IT TRUE?

The pit of Anna's stomach churned at her daughter's words. They sounded ridiculous, but Mary was never one to lie, and seemed assured of what she had seen and heard. Her mother felt her daughter's forehead and studied her eyes. "Are you sure you weren't just daydreaming? Perhaps you had too much sun out on the hillside today."

"Don't you believe an angel spoke to me? He said I was highly favored among women."

Mary's mother chuckled. "Oh, Mary. You're hardly a woman yet – you're barely into your teen years." She patted Mary's shoulder with a shake of her head.

"I'm telling the truth, Mother." Mary's voice held an edge of contention. "An angel visited me today on the hillside. A large Being wrapped in light...."

"Mary...really," her mother interrupted.

"Really, Mother. Gabriel told me I was going to conceive and bear God's Son. He even told me to name him Jesus."

"Your imagination is way too active, like all young teenage girls your age. You and your friends have talked nonstop about Messiah and being the chosen one."

"But I felt God's Presence, Mother. It surrounded me, wrapping me like a blanket. I felt covered in His amazing holy love. God gave me a child."

"Mary, you are scaring me with this talk. Did that man touch you?"

"No, Mother. Don't you understand? God, Himself has given me His Son to carry. I believe what the angel Gabriel told me. I am blessed among women and shall bear the Christ Child. Nothing is impossible with God. Don't you believe that?"

"Of course, I do, but what you're telling me is craz...."

Mary cut her mother's words short as another thought suddenly invaded her mind. "The angel also told me Cousin Elizabeth is going to have a baby."

Anna stopped wiping the table and sat down with a grave look on her face. "That's impossible. How would anyone know about Elizabeth? She is way past child-bearing age."

"Maybe I should go see her. The angel said she was already six months along."

"Maybe you should, daughter. Tell her about your dreams and visions. Maybe she will talk you out of this silly notion you have."

#

Mary was dismayed, hurt, and disappointed. She thought surely her own mother would believe her. She ran to her room and quickly jotted a note to Joseph. She rolled it into a little scroll and sealed it with a drop of wax. Tucking it into her pocket, she headed over to Hannah's home. Hannah would have to deliver her note to Marcus. She would have to trust Marcus to get the note to her betrothed and hoped Joseph would believe her – but did he even know her?

"Hannah," I need to go visit my relatives in Judea for a while." She pulled the scroll from her pocket. "Please make sure this note gets to Marcus. Tell him it is urgent that Joseph gets it right away."

"What's wrong? Why can't you give it to him next Sabbath?" Hannah asked.

"Nothing's wrong." *In fact, everything is more than right.* Mary thought as she beamed with internal pleasure. She decided it was best not to tell her friend about her experience. Sometimes Hannah talked too much. The whole town would know her news before she returned, and it wasn't ready to be shared – yet. She had to speak with Elizabeth first, then Joseph.

"I must hurry to see my cousin Elizabeth. She's almost ready to have a baby. Please?" She pushed the scroll into Hannah's hand.

"Oh, all right," Hannah said, taking the scroll. "Can I read it?" Hannah's eyes sparkled with mischief.

"No, you can't read it! It's personal, Hannah."

Hannah giggled. "Just teasing, Mary. You know I would blush over your love talk."

Mary shook her head at her friend. How could it be that her friend could seem so juvenile in just a couple of days? Or had Mary matured in how she thought and planned for her future all of a sudden?

#

The next few days were a flurry of preparation. She wanted to begin her one-hundred-mile journey toward Ain Karim as soon as possible. Her father warned her the trip could be dangerous for a woman traveling alone across the rugged dirt and rocky terrain. 'There's the possibility of bandits hiding in the mountainous regions and more,' he told her. Mary was undeterred. Her father's words would not scare her.

The little Judean village of Ain Karim where her cousin lived was five miles on the northeast side of Jerusalem. Mary hoped she would encounter a caravan that would offer some safety on her journey.

The one thing she knew beyond doubt was that God would take care of her and the precious bundle within.

———————

Luke 1:6-39

https://aleteia.org/2019/05/31/mary-traveled-a-highly-dangerous-
    path-to-visit-elizabeth

V

══════

DOUBTS & FEARS

Mary packed a few things and headed toward Judea within the week. Thinking of her father's wise advice, she packed a few extra items for the trip.

Mary's mind rolled with thoughts of the days ahead. *I must remember to take extra water. Summer days can get very hot in the lowlands.* She packed an extra shawl for the cool nights and dusty road. Excitement grew in her heart. *If God can give Elizabeth a baby in her old age, He can surely do a miracle in me. I believe you, God, for I am your handmaiden.*

"Don't go through Samaria, Mary," her father said. "It's too dangerous. Instead, travel southeast until you see the Jordan River. Follow the river's flatlands south toward Jericho. It will take you a day longer," he said, "but it will be easier and safer than traveling through Samaria. If you can make it to Salim the first day, you should find a place to stay for the night."

#

As she began the walk on the dirt road to her relative's home, her thoughts took a dark turn. Her spirit became distressed. She worried about Joseph. *What will he think when he reads my note? Will he accuse me of unfaithfulness to him? Will he bring me before the Council for judgment?*

16

Mary knew the law and the consequences of adultery. The whole town would see her as a disgrace. They may call for a public example. Stoning was the ultimate humiliation of unfaithfulness. It made her shudder. *And why should they believe me? I'm only a simple country peasant.* Mary was anxious to hear what Elizabeth would think. *Perhaps I'll stay with Elizabeth a while....*

Nearing the river, she was so absorbed watching her steps, she did not notice the two men approaching. As she looked up, she was startled to see them looking at her. She was warned to beware of bandits, but it didn't occur to her that they might attack during the daytime. Avoiding their eyes, Mary quickened her pace and hoped they would pass her without incident.

"Lord, please protect me," she whispered in her heart, "and protect your little one."

#

As Joseph nailed another board in place on his current project, his mind spun with unanswered questions. He read and re-read Mary's note, refusing to believe what it said. The words were simple and plain.

"My dear betrothed Joseph," it began.

I am with child. But you must know that I have been with no man. I am still a virgin. The child planted within my womb was placed there by God, the Father. I need you to trust me and try to understand. If you need to break the covenant between us, I won't blame you. But I pray and hope you will believe and help me raise God's Son. --Mary

Distracted as he rehearsed the words in his head, he hit his thumb with the hammer. Letting out a howl, he screamed inside. "Why, Mary? How could you do this to me? ...and how can I ever believe what you say?"

Scheduled to fix a window at Mary's parents' dwelling the next week, Joseph determined to talk with Heli, Mary's father. Perhaps taking the marriage contract back was the right thing to do. Thoughts of annulment clouded his mind.

#

Anna swept the dirt floor of their home for the fourth time, tears brimming her eyes.

"You're going to sweep down to the bedrock if you don't stop," Heli commented as he stepped through the doorway.

"I can't stop thinking of our daughter, Heli. I worry that she won't reach Elizabeth's safely. I worry that she's not in her right mind. I worry that maybe what she told me really is true. What if she is with child? What then? What would the townsfolk say? What will the rabbi and the Council do? Heli, our daughter is in grave trouble if she really is pregnant. And how will that make us look as parents?"

Anna collapsed into a nearby chair. Heli's forehead wrinkled in doubt and thought.

"Mary told you there was no man involved?"

"That is what she claims."

"Then, she's making up a story—a childhood pipedream of all Jewish girls. Just wait. You'll see. Once she talks to Elizabeth and Zachariah, they'll set her straight. As a high priest of the Davidic line, he has great wisdom and knowledge. They will give her wise counsel."

Anna dabbed her eyes. "I hope so. I want to be a grandmother, but at a more convenient time...like after Joseph is married to our daughter."

Matthew 1:18,19
Luke 1:39

VI

THE CARAVAN

The two men stopped in front of Mary, preventing her passage. At first startled, she drew upon unknown courage and gathered her wits. She demanded herself to remain calm. *Help me, God,* she prayed inwardly. Then a boldness rose up within.

"Let me pass," she said in a small but firm voice. She determined not to show any fear as she dared to look into their faces.

Their kind eyes returned her gaze, and she was reminded of the angel Gabriel. Mary's heart calmed immediately as she saw the Yakamas upon their heads and the simple Jewish garb of the working man. These men were not thieves.

"You are very young to be out on the road by yourself, Miss," said the taller man.

"Are you traveling alone?" asked the other.

Why are they speaking to me? They should know Jewish women are not allowed to communicate with strange men. She maintained her gaze but felt obligated to answer. "I am alone...." She hesitated. "...going to Jerusalem."

"That is a good three-to-five-day journey." The men gave each other a concerned look.

Mary nodded.

"We just came from Salim – about a three-hour walk down the path. We saw a caravan getting set to go south tomorrow. If you can get there before dark, perhaps you can join them. There is more safety in numbers, especially when you get to the mountainous region of Jerusalem."

She nodded again.

"In fact," the tall man said, "when you get to Salim, look up Joanna. She has an inn on the outskirts of town. Tell her Jonas and Luke sent you her way and will pay for your room when they come again next week."

Mary lifted her eyes with wonder and relief. She nodded agreement and put her hand over her heart as she slightly bowed to them in a sign of gratefulness.

The men parted allowing her to pass between them. As she did, she sensed that holy covering of God, as if His loving protection enveloped her once more. Inhaling deeply with a silent prayer of thanksgiving, she turned to thank the men again a few paces down the road.

They were gone.

Mary found Joanna's inn just as the sun sank behind the mountains. She explained to Joanna what the men had told her and secured her room for the night.

"They also told me a caravan was leaving for Jerusalem in the morning. Do you know where I can find the guide?" she asked Joanna.

Joanna nodded toward a stocky man in the corner. "The gods must be with you," she said. "He's standing right there. His name is Hiram. He's the leader and guide for the caravan."

Mary breathed another prayer of thanks. Speaking with Hiram, she assured herself a place with the caravan as far as Jerusalem. He told her to be ready to go by six o'clock in the morning.

Happy to finally rest in a secure shelter for the night, Mary relaxed. Before falling into a deep sleep, she whispered with a grateful heart, "I know it's not the 'gods' that are with me, Father. It is Yahweh. I am blessed. Blessed beyond measure by You. Thank you, for protection and giving me great favor. May I have a safe journey the rest of the way. Amen."

#

The caravan consisted mostly of men seeking to trade their wares or livestock in the villages they traveled through, culminating in Jerusalem. The few women who accompanied them were wives. A couple of small families completed the group.

Hiram, the leader and guide of the caravan, pointed toward a middle-aged woman traveling with her husband. "This is Lydia and Joab. Stay close to them," he told Mary.

The caravan started moving at a good pace.

Mary thanked him and greeted the couple. "Greetings. I'm Mary from Nazareth. Thank you for letting me accompany you."

Lydia grasped Mary's hands and drew her in. "Why are you by yourself, child? Are your parents coming?"

Mary laughed. "I *was* alone. But now it seems I'm in very good care. I'm on my way to visit my cousin just north of Jerusalem." She had to raise her voice over the bleating of the sheep close by. "I see you have goats and sheep with you."

"Yes. The goats provide good milk along the way. I've brought some cheese and nuts as well."

"And I have plenty of bread, olives, and oil that I'll gladly share."

"We've traveled with Hiram before. He is a good guide. He knows where the best encampments are along the way, and where the fresh springs are located to refill our water flasks," said Lydia.

"It seems strange to me that you and the animals are in the middle of the caravan. Why is that?" asked Mary.

"It's the safest place. Notice? The families with young children are also in the center surrounded by the men, donkeys, and camels. This way, the animals and children aren't so susceptible to prey."

"Prey?" Mary's eyes grew large in question.

"Lions. Bears. Even leopards may live in these woods in the Jordan Valley. Our animals are an enticing lunch. But the more people surrounding us, the better chance of survival."

It made a shiver creep up Mary's back. She knew they were going through a heavily wooded area lush with vegetation. But she never thought about predators.

---

https://thelayartiste.com/2019/12/14/a-photographic-journey-in-mary-and-josephs-footsteps/
https://www.bible-history.com
http://www.baptistbiblebelievers.com

VII

DANGER IN THE NIGHT

Mary's face clouded with the thought of predators surrounding her. "Don't worry, little one," Lydia soothed, noting Mary's dread. "You'll be safe with us."

The day went by without incident as the caravan followed the rocky dirt path in the lowest valley in the world. Hiram stopped at a waterhole and encouraged everyone to fill their flasks with extra water, saying it would be a distance to the next spring.

"Tomorrow, we will enter the Judean desert. We will leave the wooded valley where we've had relative shade. Stick together tonight, and don't stray too far if you need to leave camp to do your business."

After they set up a place to sleep under a large tree, Mary shared a small meal of bread, cheese, olives, and nuts with Joab and Lydia. As the sun began to hide behind the horizon, Joab went to check on his flock. In a few minutes, he ran toward Lydia with a worried look.

"One of the lambs is missing. I must find it."

"In the woods?" Alarm crossed Lydia's face.

His face was grim, but he forced a smile. "Don't worry. Others are accompanying me."

"I'm so sorry, Lydia," Mary commented. "Surely you're worried for Joab."

"Of course, but I can't tell him not to go. We are taking these sacrificial lambs to the temple in Jerusalem to sell. We can't have our pure, unblemished lambs giving up their lives before their time."

Mary put her hand to her mouth, hiding her gasp. Of course. It made more sense now. They were taking all their livestock to market. This was their business. Mary sat by the firepit in deep thought as her mind wandered. Finally, she spoke.

"That makes me sad, Lydia. These perfect, innocent lambs will have to give their lives to absolve someone else's sins with no fault of their own. Yet they will give their life so another may live forgiven."

"That's true," replied Lydia. It is Torah law for the sin offering." Lydia sighed. "I remember when my children were growing up, they wanted to name the lambs. They wanted them for pets. We cautioned against it, knowing the destiny these lambs faced. It was hard for my children to let go."

Mary looked upward at the starry expanse. "Wouldn't it be wonderful if someday one sacrifice could be made for everyone? I mean, once and for all. Just think. It would have to be a lamb so perfect and pure that everyone's sins in the whole world would be forgiven. Then no more baby lambs would have to die."

"Oh, Mary," laughed Lydia. "You're quite the dreamer, aren't you?"

"That's what Mother says, too." Mary raised her eyebrows with a sigh. "She thinks I get caught up in my daydreams."

"It is a wonderful thought, though. I agree. But how could one sacrifice be enough for everyone?" Lydia shook her head.

"I don't know," Mary admitted. "But maybe someday, that will happen."

Joab returned quite a while later holding the lamb over his shoulders.

"Are you hurt?" she asked seeing his arm bleeding. Lydia ran to him and took the lamb. Inspecting it closely for cuts or scrapes, she looked relieved.

"No blood staining the wool and no blemishes."

"Good," replied Joab. "I'm fine. We heard a lion roaring in the distance," he said breathlessly, "but we found the lamb stuck close by in the thicket. Releasing its wool was a bit of a chore, but we got away before the lion could track us."

"Are we safe? Won't the lion find us?" Mary worried. "Won't it smell food?"

"There are enough men on guard. No need to fear," said Joab.

The worried look on Joab's face told Mary a different story. As she lay on the mat in the open air, she tucked in a little closer to Lydia. Her eyes didn't close most of the night, cringing with thoughts of a lion so near.

---

https://thelayartiste.com/2019/12/14/a-photographic-journey-in-mary-and-josephs-footsteps

https://www.bible-history.com

http://www.baptistbiblebelievers.com

VIII

═══════

THE JUDEAN DESERT

Pushing off during the early morning hours, the caravan arrived at the Judean desert. By mid-morning, the sun's glare was already dancing off the steep sides of the giant, sandy dunes. The heat was becoming unbearable. A sea of sand, visible in every direction, was lifted by each breeze. Pulling her light shawl over her face helped to protect from the stinging granules. Her throat felt parched, and her lips dry.

"Drink water sparingly," Hiram had cautioned. "We will travel only as far as a Bedouin settlement and then rest during the afternoon hours because of the heat. Then, we'll set out again once the sun sets."

Between the rancid cheese or the heat of the sun, Mary suddenly became nauseous. Hurrying to the edge of the group, she hurled her breakfast onto the sand.

Lydia followed on her heels. "Mary! Are you all right?"

"Just sick to my stomach, that's all." Mary wiped her mouth with her hand and then took a sip of water from her flask.

"You looked a little pale yesterday, too. Are you sure you're not sick?"

Mary shook her head. "I'm fine, Lydia. Just the sun, I think."

The caravan turned off the path toward a small Bedouin settlement nestled along a ridge a few hours before noon. The sojourners were allowed to camp on the border a distance from the Bedouin tents where it was safest.

The men assembled makeshift shelters to protect from the sweltering sun while women prepared food. Little children from the settlement came running to pet the lambs. Their interaction with the animals and silly antics amused Mary. She didn't realize how exhausted she was from not sleeping the night before. While the others rested and ate, she found a shady place and fell sound asleep.

Hiram called out to the group as the sun began to set on another day. "Break camp and pack your belongings. Time to move."

Abruptly awakened, Mary sat up, rubbing her eyes. "I know it's cooler to travel now, but what if we get lost in the dark? Are there other reasons to travel at night?" She wanted to know as she scratched at her ankles and feet.

Joab answered her. "Hiram navigates by the stars and knows the way well. But it's also safer. We are now in desert pirate country. Bandits hide in the mountains who would love to rob us blind."

"Oh," said Mary. She had forgotten about them.

"No worries, Mary. They are less likely to attack at night," Joab continued. "Hopefully, we will arrive in Jericho by morning."

As they began the journey once again, Mary's feet itched to the bone. She stopped to remove her sandal. Giving her a foot a good scratch, she let out a little squeal at what she saw.

"Mary? What's wrong?" Lydia asked.

"My feet and ankles! They're full of red marks! And they itch like wildfire."

Lydia chuckled. "You laid down in the sand today, didn't you? Sand fleas got you. When we get to Jericho, see if you can find some eucalyptus, mint leaves, or lemons in the marketplace. We'll make an ointment to relieve your itches."

They walked all night through the desert. The cooler temperature felt refreshing after such scorching heat of the day. Mary even found she needed her shawl a few times when the breeze arose. By dawn, they had reached the edge of Jericho. And with morning came Mary's morning sickness, right on schedule.

Lydia took her husband aside. "I think that young girl is pregnant, Joab. Maybe she's all alone on this journey because she's running away."

"Oh, Lydia. You and your imagination! That's preposterous."

"No, it's my motherly instincts, husband. I know what it's like in the first trimester. Can't keep anything down. Just because she's not showing doesn't mean she's not pregnant. She's been sick since we met her."

"Only in the mornings," Joab replied.

"Exactly." Lydia gave a knowing grin.

---

https://www.travelingisrael.com/the-judaean-desert/

IX

THE MARKETPLACE

Hiram led the caravan through a high, massive gate of the caravanserai on the edge of Jericho. The roadside inn was a safe place for travelers and their animals. Those with animals stabled their donkeys and camels. Joab secured his goats and sheep on the large ground-floor courtyard. Some of the families parted company.

"There are rooms on the second floor," said Lydia. We will bunk there. It's safe. The porter secures all the doors at night."

Mary's father had suggested that she look up relatives in Jericho and stay awhile, but Mary wanted to get to Elizabeth's as soon as possible. The group would remain in Jericho for the day so travelers could replenish supplies. They would leave for Jerusalem the following morning.

"Tomorrow will be the hardest part of the journey," Lydia warned Mary. It's an uphill climb most of the way and very rocky at that. Pack extra water if you can. And don't forget the eucalyptus and lemons."

The marketplace bustled with activity as many made their last-minute purchases. Mary hurried through the booths, checking out fruit, whiffing the aroma of fresh bread, and breathing in the beautiful fragrances of different flowers. She hoped to find some grapes or other fruit that would settle her queasy stomach. Not sure why she felt so

29

sick, she decided to forego Lydia's goat milk and cheese the rest of the way.

Not finding any eucalyptus, she settled on mint leaves and purchased a couple of lemons. Another booth boasted ripe purple grapes plump with juiciness. Lifting a cluster to her nose for a whiff of sweet grapey scent, she was suddenly overcome by the mixture of all the marketplace smells. Combined with the stench of livestock and raw meat, her stomach seized once again. Mary ran behind the fruit stand and retched.

A raw smile etched across her lips as a new thought dawned. *It's really happening. The godly seed within me is starting to grow in my belly! May God be praised.*

Only one more day of traveling. Mary was thankful. She felt tired and grumpy and was anxious to see her relative, visit, and rest. It had been a long five days. Thankful that Lydia and Joab were traveling all the way to Jerusalem, she could count on them during this last trek up the mountain. Mary would take her departure just over the ridge on the northern edge of Jerusalem.

The caravan had dwindled to mostly the men going to market along with Mary, Lydia, and Joab. They turned west to climb the rocks toward Jerusalem.

"It's only about fifteen miles," Lydia told Mary, "but it's a winding path. It will take us most of the day. It's good we're getting an early start."

Mary wrinkled her forehead but nodded her understanding.

"Did you get the eucalyptus and lemons?"

"No, but I found mint leaves and lemons."

"Good. I'll mix some of the lemon juice with olive oil and squeeze the mint leaves into it. Wipe it on your feet and ankles. It will help."

The road from Jericho to Jerusalem wound its way through some of the most desolate terrain in the world. The Jericho Road was rugged, rocky, dry, and barren. Mary stumbled on some loose rocks and fell to her knees. She winced in pain but did not cry out. Doing so made her stray from Lydia's side for a few moments.

"Stay close to Lydia," Joab ordered in a brusque manner, "...and keep your face covered."

The tone of his voice made Mary quiver. "Lydia, why is he so gruff?"

"These hills and rocky chasms provide excellent hideouts for robbers and men with evil hearts," Lydia whispered. "They would most likely take advantage of a young woman such as you. It's best we keep moving and don't stop."

Mary shuddered. She didn't realize how dangerous this journey would be.

---

https://www.oikoumene.org/resources/bible-studies/the-road-through-the-wilderness

http://www.withoutexcusecreations.net

https://www.seetheholyland.net/ein-karem/

X

THE JERICHO ROAD

Mary recalled her father's warning about being watchful for bandits. But after the earlier encounter with the two generous young men, she had dismissed his words. Now, her head spun again with ideas of wild men with scabbards and swords ready to attack at any moment.

Calming herself, she thought of psalms her ancestor, King David, had written. She had memorized them in her youth.

'You are my hiding place; you protect me from trouble. You surround me with songs of victory.' 'The LORD is my strength and shield. I trust him with all my heart. He helps me.'

The climb was arduous on the young mother-to-be. Although she was strong and healthy, Mary was glad when Hiram announced they would be stopping for a lunch break.

"We are almost there," Hiram said. "Eat quickly as we must be off again to make it by mid-afternoon."

Mary found a large rock and sat down. Taking off her sandals, she rubbed her sore and blistered feet. Closing her eyes, she breathed a prayer of thanks to her heavenly Father. She took a piece of dry bread from her satchel and was about to dip it in the spiced olive oil when Joab hollered at her.

"Mary! Don't move! Sit perfectly still!"

Alarmed, Mary froze in place, her eyes staring straight ahead as he ran toward her. "When I say 'move' – get up as quickly as you can and run away from this rock," he commanded.

Her eyes widened when she saw Joab retrieve his dagger from its sheath upon his belt. Taking one rapid swipe at something behind Mary, he yelled, "NOW! MOVE!"

She let out a shriek and jumped up and away from the rock. Looking at what had been behind her made her break out in a cold sweat. There lay a headless viper, undoubtedly ready to strike.

"Lions. Unbearable heat. Bandits – and now vipers!? What else is going to threaten this trip?" Mary's words came in short breaths as she hurried towards Lydia.

Lydia snickered at her. "You forgot sandfleas and blisters. You might want to retrieve your sandals, child."

Mary gave her a scowl and cautiously retrieved her sandals and bread from the rock.

"Watch out for scorpions too. They like to hide under the rocks."

Mary tip-toed over the hot rocky road. "...and sandfleas and blisters! Ugh." She quickly put her sandals back on her feet, staying far away from the rocks. "I'll stick to the path, thank you. And I'll eat my bread on the walk."

"Only an hour or so more," Lydia said as she watched the black clouds roll in. Keep your outer cloak ready, too. It rains buckets sometimes in these hills. You might want to cover your head."

At that moment, the sky opened up as raindrops the size of grapes seemed to drop all at once. It didn't stop the caravan from moving, however. It only made the path muddy. Mary pulled her cloak around her shoulders and over her head. This would be an experience she would never forget.

As soon as the rain started, it stopped. The sun came out again to bake the Jericho Road dry. Within the next hour, the little village of Ain Karim was in sight. Mary was overjoyed.

Finally. We've arrived. She knew Zechariah and Elizabeth had a summer house in the hill country. It would only make sense that Elizabeth would retreat there where the summer breezes would cool the hot, humid days of the valley. Mary would check there first.

"Look, Lydia! How beautiful and serene it is."

"The vineyards and trees are indeed a welcome sight, aren't they? You will have a good visit with your cousin," Lydia said. "I will miss your company."

Mary hugged Lydia long and tight. "Thank you, Lydia. You'll never know how much I have appreciated your friendship and help. Thank you, Joab, for being my protection."

"Dear, sweet Mary." Lydia cupped the teenager's face in her palms. "Take care of yourself." She looked into Mary's eyes as a mother would her daughter. Then she patted Mary's stomach with a gentle touch. "And may you be blessed by this little one too."

Mary's mouth opened with surprise.

"Shhh…" Lydia put two fingers to Mary's lips. "Don't worry. I'll keep your secret."

Psalms 28:7 and 32:7 – The Living Bible

https://www.oikoumene.org/resources/bible-studies/the-road-
    through-the-wilderness

http://www.withoutexcusecreations.net

https://www.seetheholyland.net/ein-karem

XI

A WONDERFUL GREETING

Mary waved goodbye to Lydia and Joab and headed west toward the hills above Ain Karim. Nearing her cousin's place, Mary saw Elizabeth through the window kneading bread. Elizabeth's stomach bulged with child as her wrinkled face looked determined to punch the bubbles from the dough. Mary hurried inside without knocking.

"Greetings, Cousin Elizabeth!"

"Mary? Anna's girl? Could it be? My, how you've grown!" Elizabeth looked up in surprise. "Oh!" Elizabeth wrapped her arms around her own protruding belly as a wide smile broke out upon her lips. "As soon as you greeted me, the baby in my womb leaped for joy!" Elizabeth hugged the young girl.

Elizabeth, filled immediately with the Holy Spirit exclaimed loudly, "Why am I so favored that the mother of my Lord should come to visit me?"

Mary put her hand to her mouth in surprise.

Elizabeth continued, "You are blessed to believe the Lord will fulfill His promises to you. Blessed are you among women, and blessed is the Child you will bear!"

How would Elizabeth know unless God had told her? Tears welled in Mary's eyes with new realization and the inspiration of truth. *'The mother of my Lord,' she said. 'Blessed among women,' she said.* Mary squeezed her eyes tight to prevent the tears from flowing, but her heart exploded with joy and adoration to God. She crossed her hands over her bosom and began to worship.

"Oh, how my soul praises the Lord. How my spirit rejoices in God my Savior! For he took notice of his lowly servant girl."

She lifted her eyes toward heaven with renewed faith and determination.

"From now on, all generations will call me blessed, for the Mighty One is holy, and he has done great things for me. He shows mercy from generation to generation to all who fear him. His mighty arm has done tremendous things! Holy is His name...."

#

Mary stayed in Judea for another three months helping Elizabeth prepare for the birth of her first child. She reveled in God's power when Cousin Zechariah could miraculously speak again after naming baby John. That was a wonderful day, indeed.

When all the neighbors and nearby relatives arrived for the naming and circumcision ceremony on the eighth day, they were sure the baby would be named after his father. After all, that was the custom. But Elizabeth said, "No! His name will be John!" They were confused, for no one else in the family had that name. They decided to ask Zechariah. He motioned for a writing tablet. To everyone's surprise, he wrote, "His name is John." Instantly Zechariah could speak again, and he began praising God.

Awe fell upon the whole neighborhood and the news of what had happened spread throughout the Judean hills. "What is this child destined to be?" The whole community wanted to know.

When it was time for Mary to leave for home, she knew Elizabeth would be in good hands. So many friends, neighbors, and relatives were happy for her and knew God's favor was on this miracle child. She pondered all the wisdom and advice her cousin had given.

#

In some ways, she couldn't wait to see her parents and friends again. In other ways, she dreaded it. With a bubble beginning to form in her own belly, Mary knew she would eventually have to face the townspeople of Nazareth. And, she would have to talk to Joseph. Somehow, she had to find out what Joseph thought. And that terrified her.

Please, God. Speak to Joseph. Show him how to help me raise this Holy One. I trust You to protect me and direct my paths.

God had proved through Elizabeth that He could do what was physically impossible. Mary trusted that God would also make a way for her. He always did. Not sure of all that lay ahead, Mary knew this: she was blessed and she was chosen. She promised to serve God to the best of her ability as the mother of His Son.

See Luke 1:39-66

XII

═══════════

JOSEPH'S DILEMMA

Meanwhile, back in Nazareth, Joseph struggled with his own dilemma. Confusing thoughts collided with conflicting emotions contemplating Mary's note, his feelings for her, and what he had vowed. Being an honorable man, he would dutifully follow through with his commitment to his vows. He had promised them a year's worth of maintenance. *Whatever happens, I will do what I promised. But what do Mary's parents really think? Had she told them? Did they believe her story?*

Joseph knocked on the door, and then entered the home of Anna and Heli. He was met with the aroma of freshly-baked date cakes.

"Joseph, greetings! Good to see you this sunny day!" Anna put a warm cake on a plate and offered it to him.

He waved it away. "Good day, Anna," Joseph replied without emotion. "Is Heli around?"

"Still in the field. What's wrong? You look so downcast."

"My body is well," he said. "But my heart breaks." He stopped and looked into her eyes. Is it true, Anna? ...about Mary?"

Anna diverted her eyes to the window and feigned ignorance. "What do you mean? What about Mary?"

Joseph noticed how her tone turned to ice and she refused to look at him. "I haven't seen her for weeks – at synagogue or in the market-place. Where is she?"

"Mary is in Judea for a few months helping her cousin get ready for the birth of her child."

Joseph showed some sense of relief. "Well..." he exhaled deeply, "that explains her absence."

He went to work on the project for the day and no more was said about Mary, or anything else. He decided not to press Anna any further. She seemed distraught simply talking about her daughter. After he'd finished with repairs, he put away his tools. "When will Heli be home? I need to talk to him."

"He'll be home by sundown."

Joseph looked toward the sky. That wouldn't be for a couple of hours yet. He would have to return another day.

"Does Heli still have the marriage contract?"

She nodded with a curious look. "Why?"

"Tell him I might need it."

Joseph felt disappointed and betrayed. He had planned on getting the contract today, but he'd have to wait until the next week when he returned. He'd make sure Heli was home, and then, he would get the document, tear it up, and nullify the marriage. *I'll move away from Nazareth. Everything will be done quietly without any public disgrace to Mary or her family.* He played out the events in his tormented mind.

On his way out the door, he turned and saw Anna with her head in her hands. He suspected she already knew what he knew.

The more Joseph thought about tearing up the contract and getting away from the whole situation, the more constricted he became. He began to think about Mary and the dilemma she faced. He might be able to end the marriage quietly and leave, but that wouldn't stop her from having the child.

Joseph knew the dire consequences Mary would have to face if she was allowed to go full-term. Because she was betrothed to him, she would be punished and ostracized as an adulterer. By law, Mary could even be stoned for her illicit actions. *Who would believe that she was carrying the Son of God? They would doubt she was still a virgin. Who would believe in immaculate conception?* A chill went through Joseph's bones. *How can I believe?*

"God, what do you want me to do?" his heart cried out. "The child is not mine. Is she lying to me?" Mary's reputation was chaste and honorable. She would not prostitute herself or bring shame to her family intentionally. *Was she raped and too afraid to tell the truth? Maybe she is out of her mind and that's why she was sent away for a while.* "I don't want her to go through this trauma alone," he prayed. "Lord, what am I to do?"

Abruptly, another thought invaded his mind. *Is the child she carries really divine? Can it really be possible? All she asked was that I trust her.*

"I want to. God, I really want to."

Matthew 1:19

XIII

JOSEPH'S ANSWER

Joseph fell into a fitful sleep that night as he thought of Mary's problem and how it would affect their lives. Then, an angel appeared to him in his dream.

"Don't fear to take Mary as your wife," the angel told him. Then the most amazing announcement of all saying, "The child she carries is truly from the Holy Spirit. Mary will bear God's Son, and you are to name him Jesus because he will save his people from their sins."

The angel continued, "This has happened so that what the prophet Isaiah said will be fulfilled: 'Behold, a virgin shall be with child, and shall bring forth a son, and they shall call his name Emmanuel, which being interpreted is, God with us.'"

Joseph awoke with a start. The dream seemed so real, and for the first time, with wonderful new revelation, he believed Mary. *I don't understand, but I will choose to believe. I choose to trust. And I choose to obey.*

A new thought popped into Joseph's mind. *If I take Mary for my wife now in her early stages of pregnancy, the townsfolk will think the baby is mine. I will bear the disgrace. The brunt of any accusations of impropriety will be on me when the baby comes early.*

\#

Arriving at his future in-law's house a week later, a serious-looking Anna met Joseph at the door. "Come," she said quietly with downcast eyes. "Heli is in the inner room."

Joseph followed the older woman into the inner room where Heli reclined. Seeing Joseph, he stood to his feet.

"Joseph, greetings," his tone was solemn. "I have been told you would come." He walked over to the small chest on the upper shelf. "I have the wedding contract here."

Heli took the document from its hiding place and tried to hand it to Joseph. Joseph shook his head and motioned for Heli to put it back. A peculiar twinkle shone from Joseph's eye. "It's not what you think, Heli. I don't want the document. I've changed my mind."

"But Anna thought...."

"I know. And it's true; my thoughts went that direction. I was ready to call for a quiet divorce from Mary and nullify this covenant."

"Then you know – about Mary, I mean," said Heli.

"Yes. I've known for almost three months now. Mary sent me a note. I know she doesn't lie. I believe what she said is true." Joseph paused a minute as he stroked his beard. "Tell me something, Heli."

Mary's father wrinkled his forehead in confusion as he tucked the paperwork back into its safe place. He gave Joseph a questioning look.

A slight grin crossed Joseph's lips. "Does the Torah demand that we wait a full year between the signing of the covenant and the wedding feast?

"It is customary to wait a full twelve months between the betrothal and the wedding feast. That gives the groom time to prepare a place for his bride and to work off the dowry. It also gives the bride time to prepare herself for the wedding." Heli scratched his head. "But it's not law. It is up to me, her father, to say when the bridegroom can come for his bride." A wry smile began to creep across Heli's lips. "...why?"

I want to take Mary to be my wife now," Joseph said. "That is... as soon as she returns from Judea."

Heli's chest raised as he heaved a huge breath. He was silent for several minutes. "Nothing would make me happier." Heli's face showed relief and joy. He gave Joseph a fatherly slap on the back.

"Wonderful," Joseph's face glowed with pleasure. "As soon as Mary gets home, send word that she's back. God willing, I will come within the week and take her to my home. I will prepare the marriage feast. Tell her to be ready and listen for the shofar to sound!"

―――――――――

Matthew 1:19-24

XIV

MARY'S RETURN

Mary returned to Nazareth after a three-month stay in the Judean hill country. She was blessed to find another caravan traveling north. Now in her second trimester, her morning sickness had almost subsided. She felt a little stronger and more mentally prepared for the journey.

Arriving home, Mary ran to hug her mother, but Anna held her daughter at arm's length. She scowled noticing the small bulge protruding under Mary's loose tunic.

"So, it is true. You're going to have a baby," Anna said. "What did Elizabeth and Zechariah have to say about that?"

Mary detected the disappointment in her mother's voice. Taking her mother by the arms, she led her to a bench. "Mother, sit down. You need to hear what I was told. When I greeted Cousin Elizabeth, she said baby John leaped within her womb. She was filled with the Holy Spirit. She called me 'the mother of her Lord and that I was blessed among all women. She said I was blessed to believe all God had said.'"

Anna's face reddened. "And what did Cousin Zechariah say?"

"Zechariah didn't speak. He couldn't speak. He was struck dumb by the angel because he didn't believe the angel's message that Elizabeth was going to have a child. In fact, he couldn't speak the whole nine months of Elizabeth's pregnancy!" He could only communicate by writing on a tablet. But when it came time to name the baby, his tongue was miraculously loosed, and he could speak again."

Mary went on to explain the other things Elizabeth said. "Mother, if God can produce a miracle baby for them, don't you think He can surely give me a child by supernatural means?"

"Mary…Mary. I just…don't…know…how."

"That's the beauty of faith and trust. I chose to believe the angel Gabriel's proclamation– a holy message from God. He honored my belief. Mother – God chose me, a simple Jewish girl with no fame or notoriety. I am still a virgin, Mother, and the baby I carry is God's Son – the Messiah. I have simple belief and trust in the Almighty God who can do anything."

Anna shook her head. But she could not deny that Mary was indeed with child.

Mary wrapped her arms around her mother's neck. "I know what you must think. I have had questions too. But I believe God will work it all out for good. You'll see. He has a grand plan. We just don't know all the details yet."

"You have matured far beyond your years, Mary. In only three short months, your wisdom and insight exceed mine."

Mary patted her mother's shoulders, "Thank you, Mother. I only want yours and Father's blessing for this child."

"You are aware Joseph has many questions as well."

Mary bit her lip. "I'm sure he does."

"He asked your father about the marriage contract. It sounded like he wanted to break the covenant."

A look of sorrow swept across Mary's face as her shoulders dropped. "What did Father say?"

"You'll have to speak to him."

She could hardly wait until her father came in from the field to ask him. Beside herself with hope and expectation, combined with doubts and fears, she tried to busy herself to distract from worry.

Her father had not said much to her about her condition, yet she knew he loved and supported her. He was also a very devout Jew who followed the Law to every jot and tittle. *...much like Joseph,* she thought wryly.

While setting the table for the evening meal, she saw her father coming up the road. Quickly setting the bowls upon the table, she rushed out the door to meet him.

"Father!" Mary wrapped her arms around his neck like she did when she was a little girl.

"How's my Mary-girl?" He squeezed her in return. "I'm so glad you're back safely."

"Father! I can't wait any longer. Mother said Joseph talked with you. Please, what did he say? I have to know whether it's good or bad."

Heli's grin was wide. His countenance spoke approval and acceptance as he gazed upon his eager daughter. "First things first," he said, patting his own stomach. "First, we eat. Then we speak."

Mary knew better than to argue. She fidgeted through the whole meal. She shared some of her experiences on her travels to and from Judea.

Anna was curious as well. Heli hadn't told her anything about his meeting with Joseph, and it wasn't her place to ask.

Satisfied and full, Heli leaned back in his chair after everything was cleaned and cleared.

"Sit, ladies. I wanted you both together to hear what I have to say. Now, we talk."

Mary sat in rapt attention before him. She was hopeful...

"Mary—" Heli kept his face stern and paused for effect.

"Yes, Father?" She leaned in to hear his words.

"You will need to prepare your lamps and other belongings..." Heli spoke slowly and distinctly.

Is he sending me away? Mary wondered.

"Stay ready, Mary..." her father continued with a quick wink and loving smile. "...for any day now, you might hear the sound of the shofar."

Mary knew what that meant. She jumped from her chair. "...and Joseph is going to come for me? And take me to his home?" Mary's voice rose with excitement and joy with each word. Her heart began to flutter.

"But, Heli," interjected Anna. "It's not been a full year yet. Is it legal?"

"The Torah says the father must approve, and I do. As long as the father gives approval, yes, it's legal."

Anna nodded her approval as the worry lines disappeared from her brow.

"That's what Joseph wanted to talk about," continued Heli. "He's been preparing you a place, Mary, and getting everything ready for the marriage feast. He is only awaiting word from me as to when he can come to get you. The question is – are you ready?"

Mary twirled on her feet. "YES! A thousand times, yes! Thank you again, sweet Lord!" She lifted her face upward. "I knew You would work everything out!"

Luke 1: 39-45

https://bibleandrevelation.com/2017/08/08/the-ancient-jewish-wedding/

XV

━━━━━━

THE WEDDING FEAST

Mary's joy was boundless. She praised God in spirit and song. The Babe within her womb quickened. It made Mary jump and then smile. *Do you approve, little one?* She rubbed the small bump. *I promise to be a good wife, and a good mom.* The real union would be way ahead of schedule. She wouldn't have to wait long.

She was expected to trim her lamps, fill them with oil and prepare her other things to move to the home of her husband-to-be. The next three days were packed with preparations. Mary couldn't wait to tell Hannah. They had so much to catch up on – but she felt checked in her spirit against telling Hannah about the baby. She would find out soon enough. In the meantime, Hannah could help with the wedding preparations.

Joseph was also busy with events. His friend Marcus helped him finish the special room where he and Mary would complete their wedding vows. Friends and relatives were notified of the coming wedding day.

Mary wasn't privy to the day nor the time when Joseph would come for her. She simply had to be ready at any time for the shofar to sound. It would announce his coming. Mary felt a tremble of excitement as she thought of that day.

#

A couple of weeks after coming back home, she awakened one morning with a tingling in her body. The sun seemed to shine with new brilliance and the air smelled sweet. Maternally massaging her belly, she stopped and listened closely. There seemed to be electricity in the air.

Will it be today? She didn't have to wait long to find out.

Shortly before the sun moved directly overhead, Mary heard a distant blast of the shofar. She ran outside to check the road. Its tone was clear and getting louder. If Joseph left from his home and walked to hers, that meant he'd be there within twenty minutes.

She squealed with overflowing joy! "He's coming! He's coming for me!" Mary hurried to pull on her wedding dress, thankful that her mother let out the seams so that it billowed around her and hid the baby bump.

While she pinned up her hair, her mother lay a sheer overlaying cloak over her shoulders and placed her embroidered veil on her head. "They're almost here, Mary. Are you ready?"

"Mother! I am so happy…and thankful for the man God has given me. And yes, I am ready!"

Leading the entourage, Joseph was dressed in the traditional white tunic representing purity. Following him, the wedding party and guests sang and danced their way to Mary's home announcing the groom's arrival.

With much fanfare, Joseph stopped before Mary's house where she excitedly waited inside. Turning to the guests, his face lit up in a wide smile. As they began to rejoice and clap, he entered her home.

Joseph was taken aback by her youthful beauty. Mary's face was radiant and pure. This was the first time he'd seen her since the Kiddushin, but then her face was veiled. He was enthralled as she gave him a sweet smile and looked into his eyes with trust. This was his bride. Her cheeks glowed a warm pink under his gaze and his heart quickened.

I will take care of her, Lord, he whispered the silent prayer, *...and her child.* A sudden calm of assurance came upon Joseph's heart, and he knew he was doing the right thing by marrying this girl who claimed to be impregnated by God Himself.

He gave Mary a loving smile as she stood expectantly waiting, looking up at him. Joseph picked her up in his arms and carried her across the threshold to the party waiting outside.

When he set her down outside, the wedding party broke out in celebration, clapping, laughing, and cheering. Singing accompanied the group as they danced their way through the village back to Joseph's home.

Joseph and Mary wove their way through the crowd dancing while greeting and thanking people for coming to witness their special day. Throughout the afternoon the festivities went on with the wine blessing, the vows, and the couple being raised upon chairs in ceremonial flavor.

A large wedding feast had been prepared for the guests while a special private meal was ready for Joseph and Mary behind closed doors in the special room Joseph had prepared for his bride. The intimacy in sharing their first meal together face to face was considered sacred and holy.

It was finally time for them to enter the bedroom chamber together. Closing the door symbolized their union as man and wife. Jewish tradition dictated they share a meal and then consummate their marriage vows. Their guests would remain outside as virtual witnesses of this event.

As Joseph closed the door, he looked at Mary with adoration in his eyes. She blushed but gave him a sweet smile.

Her body trembled slightly as he removed her veil and outer cloak. He wrapped his arms around her and kissed her on the forehead.

"My dear, sweet Mary," he whispered softly in her ear. "How brave you've been."

"I will honor you, Joseph, for all of my days. Your belief in me and in God's Word means the world to me. I know He will bless you for your faithfulness."

It felt so good to finally be able to talk face to face. She looked up meekly at Joseph as he held her close. Mary knew what was supposed to happen next but wasn't sure quite what to expect.

Joseph's eyes misted for a moment. He gazed upon his young wife with new respect, honor, and love. With a warm and gentle squeeze, he said, "It is customary to consummate the marriage now, and that is what we are going to let our guests think. But in your condition, I will honor you and the child. We will wait until after the baby is born."

Mary leaned her head against Joseph's chest in love and appreciation, so thankful for his selflessness.

"You are an honorable man, dear husband. I love you."

"And I love you," he said as he hugged her tight.

---

https://www.myjewishlearning.com/article/ancient-jewish-marriage/

https://www.myjewishlearning.com/article/after-the-wedding-ceremony/

https://free.messianicbible.com/feature/ancient-jewish-wedding-customs-and-yeshuas-second-coming/

XVI

DECREE

Over the next few months, Mary settled into Joseph's home, loving every minute as his new wife. As the Child within her grew, she spent more time at home and away from the public. Since the marriage, her mother finally warmed up to the idea of becoming a grandmother.

Joseph came through the door one day with a frown of disgust on his face. "Heard disturbing news today," he said as he washed his hands. "Talk about town says the Emperor wants to number the people. You know what our people think about that!"

Mary thought a moment and nodded. "The prophet Hosea said, 'Yet the Israelites will be like the sand on the seashore, which cannot be measured or counted.'"

"It is strictly forbidden by our Talmud! It could bring judgment on the Jews. It worries me, Mary."

"Why would the great Emperor of Rome need an accounting of the people?" she wondered.

"Word has it that it's much deeper than just knowing how many citizens are in the Empire. Although that is a prized objective, he wants a poll tax too."

Mary's ire rose, surprising herself with her outburst. "He doesn't have enough money in the coffers without extorting from us commoners?

He thinks he's our god, and people treat him as such. Just look at one of the coins engraved with his image."

Joseph flipped over the coin he had in his hand. "'Caesar Augustus, Son of a god' is inscribed on it. What an ego!"

"He'd better be careful," Mary's tone warned, "or he will anger the one true God. Soon he and everyone else will know what a real Son of God looks like." She bit her lip with determination and grit.

"Careful, Mary...that timing is not in our hands," Joseph warned. "I'm sure we'll find out more about this census soon."

Another month and a half passed with more scuttlebutt rumored about a census throughout the region. Joseph learned that Caesar Augustus wanted a public registry not only to count the people but to distinguish his Roman citizens for military purposes. For everyone registered, an oath of allegiance to Rome and to Rome's self-acclaimed god would be required.

Nearing the end of the year, Rome's planning and implementation of Roman books needed to be reconciled. Taxes were due. Palestine was the only region that had not been accounted for yet. Augustus put out a decree that everyone would have to travel to the city of their ancestors' origin to register.

As Mary entered her ninth month, her mother talked nonstop about helping deliver the baby. She was visiting Mary the day the town crier came through Nazareth proclaiming the decree.

Joseph came home with a worried look. "A decree went out today throughout the village," he said. "Everyone must return to their own city to sign the registry and pay their taxes."

"Can't you pay it here, in Nazareth?" Anna asked.

"Not this time. The decree dictates that each one must go to the city of their lineage. My family is from the tribe of Judah – the Davidic line. So, for me, that is Bethlehem, the city of David."

"That's also true for me," said Mary. "Our family also is of the royal lineage of King David. We have the same heritage."

"But Mary, you can't go," her mother said with consternation. "The baby is due any time now. Surely Joseph can sign for both of you."

"She's right, Mary," agreed Joseph. "You're too far along for such a grueling journey."

"We both have to go, Joseph," Mary insisted. "Aren't we both under penalty of law if we don't? You could lose your business or property—or worse if we don't comply. When's the deadline?"

"We have until the end of the year."

"That's only three weeks away," Anna said.

"Then we had better start making preparations to leave within the next few days," Mary said.

Both Joseph and Anna gave her a stern 'no' look.

Mary simply smiled. "We'll take it slow and easy, Mother. I'm healthy and strong. The baby is strong – He is God's Son, after all. And remember what the prophet Micah said?"

Anna just shook her head at her stubborn daughter.

Joseph's eyes lit up as a light dawned in his memory. "But you, Bethlehem Epaphras, who are small among the clans of Judah, out of you will come forth for Me a ruler of Israel...."

"Don't you see?" Mary's face shone with revelation. "Bethlehem is where I must be to have this baby. God, His Father will get me there safely. He's working it all out! It's meant to be."

Matthew 1, Luke 1, 2; Hosea 10:1; Micah 5:2

http://theodds.website/an-unusual-roman-census-decree-by-caesar-augustus/

http://theodds.website/nazareths-town-crier-proclamation-that-changed-history/

RE: Caesar Augustus- http://chabad.org

http://Nationalgeographic.org

http://Brittanica.com

Josephus, *Antiquities of the Jews*

XVII

THE LONG JOURNEY

For a journey that normally took four to five days, Mary and Joseph planned a full week of travel. Only a few miles of walking a day for the mother-to-be. Joseph said he didn't want to deliver the baby by the roadside. Mary kept telling him not to worry, God had it all planned out. She would get to Bethlehem on time.

With many people on their way to Jerusalem to pay taxes and register for the census, the couple had no problem finding a caravan. The first day carried them to the foothills of Mt. Gilboa where they camped by the river.

Much grumbling was heard amongst the crowd of the oppressive rule of the Roman government under Caesar Augustus, and that of King Herod closer to home. While they ate their evening meal, Joseph and Mary overheard some of the men talking.

"I heard this census was being taken so the Emperor could know who had ancestral rights to his throne," said one man.

"He wants to protect his reign at any cost," said another. "He won't hesitate to eliminate anyone who thinks about taking it away."

"Same goes for King Herod. He's ruthless."

Someone else spoke. "That's not the worst part. The government takes our money and then spends it on special interests. They have a party and then say it's a sacrificial offering to their Roman god, Mars!"

"Isn't he the god who supposedly avenged the Emperor's uncle, Julius Caesar?"

"The same. 'It's on behalf of the citizens,' they say, 'to ensure good health and wealth.'" The older man spat on the ground. "Pagans. Makes me sick."

"We need a savior to avenge us from this tyrannical rule," the first man mused.

"You're a dreamer," replied the other. "I'm afraid no one is coming to save us."

Mary gave Joseph a knowing look. "I wish we could tell them...."

The journey had been long and tedious. They had enough provisions, and Mary insisted she could handle the duress. Joseph had promised to take it slow for Mary's sake. They had already walked for seven days, stopping way too many times along the ninety-mile-long trek. They only had to make it over the mountainous path from Jericho to Jerusalem and then south to the hillside 'city of bread,' Bethlehem.

Mary didn't want to tell her new husband that her pains were coming faster and with more intensity the farther she walked. They were also coming with good regularity. Suddenly a sharp pain doubled her over. She grabbed her belly and looked away so Joseph wouldn't see her face. Waiting it out, she inwardly prayed. *Help, Lord. Please get me to Bethlehem tonight. Please, work everything out.*

But he saw. He watched her catch her breath. He worried the winding uphill terrain ahead might prove too hard for her, but she insisted she could travel on.

Recalling the surroundings, Mary saw the rock where the viper almost bit her only six months before. "Sorry. I must rest a minute."

As Joseph helped ease her onto the nearby rock, Mary noticed the worry etched deep into his forehead. "Don't worry, Joseph. I'll be fine. " Mary grimaced as yet another pain took her breath away. Bending over, she grabbed the sides of the rock.

Joseph's heart melted with emotion. He wanted to help Mary but didn't know how. His young wife knew the rigors of this dangerous trip, yet she insisted upon coming. His desire was to leave her in Nazareth where she could birth the child around family. But law demanded they register together.

Watching in dismay as many travelers passed them by, he worried that they had lost valuable time. It was already late afternoon. He had to get Mary to a place where she could lay down. A man passed with a burro in tow.

"Sir?" he asked as he approached the man. "Would you consider selling me your burro?" He glanced Mary's way. "My wife has need of it."

Kindness flooded his eyes upon seeing Mary heavy with child. "I don't need the burro," he said. "You can have her. Let the mother ride the rest of the way."

Joseph thanked the man, and they were on their way again. At the top of the Mount of Olives, Joseph breathed in the fresh air. "Look, Mary. You can see Jerusalem from here! Downhill through the Kidron Valley, and we will be there. Why don't we stay in Jerusalem tonight where you can lay down and rest? You are so weary; I can see it in your eyes. Then, tomorrow we'll go to Bethlehem."

Mary shifted her weight over the burro. She shook her head. "No...Jos..eph." Her words came in short pants. "Bethlehem is...only five miles...more."

"And all uphill. I'm not sure you're up to it."

"Joseph," her eyes pleaded as her pains temporarily subsided. "We have to make it to Bethlehem. Tonight. God's Son must be born there. Please."

------

https://carm.org/evidence-and-answers/would-joseph-really-have-had-to-travel-to-bethlehem-for-a-census/

https://truthbook.com/jesus/mary-mother-of-jesus/mary-travels-to-bethlehem/

http://thebiblejourney.org; http://livius.org; http://brittanica.com

Josephus, *Antiquities of the Jews*

XVIII

PONDERINGS IN THE STABLE

By late night, the couple finally reached Bethlehem. Joseph was beside himself the whole way. By going around Jerusalem instead of through the city, they made a little better time. But Mary didn't have much longer before the baby would be born.

They had no reservations, family, or friends in town. They had to take their chances at finding a place to stay. From place to place they asked, but the answer was always the same, "Sorry, we're full. You should have come earlier." Every home had its own relatives filling it. No room for visitors.

Joseph didn't favor staying at the caravanserai, the roadside inn for caravan travelers. But he didn't want Mary to deliver this baby in the cold and dark outside either. There was no place left to ask. He asked God for guidance.

Joseph met the manager of the inn at the gate. Behind him, Joseph noticed the many people already crowded in the rooms. "Please," he pleaded. "My wife needs to lie down. Her pains are great, and the child is soon to come."

The man looked back toward the inn, raucous with laughter and drinking men, then at the young girl bent over the burro's neck, gripping the mane with one hand, holding her stomach with the other. Shaking his head he said, "Between people being here for the Feast of Trumpets and others for the registry, I've already let too many in tonight. You wouldn't want your wife with this rowdy crowd."

He scratched his head with a scowl on his face as Joseph began to turn away. "Wait. It's nothing much, but there's a small space underneath the inn by the animals," he pointed with his head. "Best I can do." He shrugged his shoulders. "No charge," he added over his shoulder and went back inside.

Joseph had other thoughts about the innkeeper while he led the burro down the path and into the cave beneath the inn. He tried to sound cheerful. "At least it's inside and out of the rain," he told Mary as he helped her off the burro.

Bunching the hay into a makeshift bed, he put his robes over top of the hay and helped Mary lay down as her body contorted with another contraction.

Her pains subsided, giving her a moment's respite. She gave him a weak but grateful smile and relaxed a minute. But her mind spun as her thoughts tumbled in her tired brain. *Highly favored among women? In a stinky stable with the animals? I never imagined it would be like this.* She leaned back on the surrounding hay and sighed with a slight twinge of guilt for her questioning. *I am your handmaiden, Lord. But why here? Why now?*

"Ooooh..." she groaned, drawing her knees upward. She poked at the straw to smooth out a more comfortable space when another pain wrenched her body. She arched her back to subdue the pain to no avail. "Ooooh!" She bent over with contractions minutes apart. *Lord, I'm afraid. Is it really supposed to hurt this bad?*

"Fear not." The angel's words rung in her head.

"Mary, what can I do to help?" Joseph rushed to her side. "Are you cold? More blankets? I'll see if we have any more." Running back to where he'd dropped the baggage and provisions, he rummaged through their belongings.

With a few minutes of respite between contractions, Mary admired her new husband busying himself with unnecessary things like a nervous father-to-be. *Kind, wonderful Joseph. What a godly and upright man. The baby isn't even his, yet he's given me everything.*

As Joseph returned with more blankets in hand, she smiled in spite of the pain. *I'm so thankful Joseph came around to believe that my son is truly God's Son. He will be a good father.*

"I brought the swaddling cloths too," he said as he tucked the blankets around her.

She gazed through the opening of the dark little stable where they had found refuge. Mary marveled at God's handiwork in the skies. *Even the heavens know Someone special is coming into the world tonight! Joseph may need the extra light to help deliver this baby.*

Mary remembered what her cousin Elizabeth told her about her child, *'He shall be great, and shall be called the Son of the Highest. The Lord God shall give him the throne of his father David and he shall reign over the house of Jacob forever. Of his kingdom there shall be no end,' she had said. What does it all mean?*

Mary's ponderings were interrupted as she was taken by another sharp contraction. Breathing quickened as perspiration broke out on her brow. Mary's breaths came in quicker pants. Her back felt like it would break in two.

"Joseph..." she whispered through her agony. "It's time...I need your help...."

Luke 2:4-6

XIX

THE LIGHT OF THE WORLD

Joseph helped the Babe enter the world and both marveled at his first cry. Beams of brilliant starlight suddenly streamed through the stable window, haloing the holy infant in Joseph's arms.

"Look, Mary. Your Son."

Mary took the soft cloths nearby and wrapped the first Christmas gift given to man. Settling back on the straw, she closed her eyes in sweet relief and joy. With the Baby in her arms, Mary whispered, "Thank you, God, for this wonderful Child. He is Yours." Looking up at Joseph, her eyes spoke of relief, happiness, and gratefulness.

"Thank you, sweet Joseph, for being with me and helping deliver this Child." Her words faded as the new mother gave the Baby back to Joseph to lay in the manger. She lay back to rest and was soon asleep.

Joseph's soul was warmed. He was thankful, too.

As Mary slept, Joseph's mind traveled back to a few months before. His thoughts had wrestled in torment what to do with Mary and the whole situation. He had been so conflicted.

Now the Baby was here. They would be just fine, so matter what other people might think. Thankfulness filled his heart as he gazed down upon his wife. His heart melted with love at the sight of her peaceful countenance.

Mary had known the consequences of her actions, yet she willingly accepted them. The village thought she had gone mad. It had appeared her parents sent her away for a while.

She had claimed it was God's doing from the start. She said the Child was God's special gift to the world and that she had been chosen by Him to bear His Son. She told me she was scared but didn't ask for pity – or forgiveness. She only wanted my understanding. "Please, just trust me," she had said. "I only need you to believe me and believe God."

The Child began to whimper. Joseph gently lifted the Babe from the manger. As he stroked the baby's fuzzy hair, the Baby looked into Joseph's eyes. *Am I only imagining a look of approval?* The baby nuzzled into Joseph's chest and closed his eyes.

I'm glad I obeyed the angel and took Mary for my wife. I won't regret my actions. God needs me to help raise His Son. The brilliant light from the huge star shone about the Child in illuminating radiance. Rocking the Babe in his arms, Joseph let his wife rest while he sat in awe with his thoughts.

Mary awoke with the light in her eyes. "Did I sleep all night? It's so bright!"

Her heart was content as she watched Joseph holding and rocking the Baby in his arms. Joseph would help her, and they would be all right. She rolled over and looked through the open window. The night sky was sprinkled with light. But one star was so bright that it shone with the brightness of twenty combined.

"Look, Joseph! It's as if Heaven itself is announcing His birth! All the stars seem to be converging together into one big army. Look how bright! All Heaven is celebrating! Over there above the ridge!"

"You are an amazing young woman, Mary," Joseph's voice held admiration and awe. "Truly, you are blessed among all women. I will do my best to help you raise the Messiah. I will teach Him what I know and help guide His path in the ways of Jewish tradition." The Babe stirred in Joseph's arms. "I think He's hungry," Joseph said, handing Him to Mary.

"I am blessed by you, dear Joseph," Mary gave him a loving look. "I know you will help me. But what now?" She smoothed the baby's hair and kissed his forehead as she prepared to nurse him.

"You should rest right now and not worry. God will take care of the details – isn't that what you said? In the meantime, I will try to find a better place to stay in Bethlehem other than this stinky stable. I believe we should stay here until time for your purification rites."

After Mary nursed the Babe, Joseph lay the contented Christ Child in the empty stone watering trough where he'd placed some soft hay to cushion its hardness. The light of the star glowed around the Babe in majestic beams.

"Look, Mary," Joseph said in amazement. "The Light of the World."

Luke 2:6,7
John 8:12; 9:5

XX

───────

GOD'S LAMB

When Mary and Joseph awakened the next morning, they were startled as several shepherds burst into the stable.

Wild-eyed with wonder and awe written on their faces, the oldest-looking member of the group pointed toward the sleeping baby. "There he is! Just as the angel said!"

"...lying in a manger," said the youngest.

"Forgive us, please. We cannot contain our joy or excitement this morning after what we experienced last night, and then now to find it's really true! I'm Nathaniel. These are my sons, Joshua and Micah."

Mary nodded. Joseph welcomed them.

Their joy was evident as they spoke of Baby Jesus. "Look, the baby is tightly bound in swaddling clothes. The angel said that would be a sign to us," said Joshua. "...like he is God's lamb."

"This is how the priests wrap the pure, unblemished lambs," explained Nathaniel.

"And they lay that lamb in these stone feeding troughs – the manger – for safe-keeping and protection until they are ready for sacrifice," continued Joshua. "That was the second sign for us to see."

Startled at their words, Mary covered her open mouth. She had just laid the Baby down for a nap. Yet, in the boisterousness of the shepherds, He slept sound.

"Tell me," Mary said quietly. "How did you know to come here?"

"The angel told us!" Excitement lit up Joshua's eyes as he repeated the event. The angel said, 'You will find a baby wrapped in swaddling cloths and lying in a manger.'"

Micah added with a grin, "Where else would we find you? This is the only stable in Bethlehem with mangers."

"Where did you come from?" asked Joseph.

"We are shepherds in the Judean hill country," said Nathaniel. "Most shepherds must keep sheep away in the wilderness, but we raise pure lambs to sell to the temple suitable for sacrifice. Bethlehem is known for the purest, most unblemished lambs. We were watching our flock last night when suddenly there was an explosion of light in the sky. We were blinded by it. Then the angel appeared."

Micah jumped in. "We were all terrified! We thought we must have done something wrong with the lambs!"

Nathaniel laughed at his son. "Maybe that's what *you* thought. Is there something you need to confess, Micah?"

Micah hung his head and blushed. "Well, anyway, I was scared out of my wits. But then the angel said in a loud voice, "Fear not."

He's been saying that a lot lately, Mary thought. *God comes down to show us Himself and His love, and the best response we can give is fear. Lord, teach us to trust you more.*

At that moment, the Child stirred and awoke. Mary put clean wraps on Him, and then picked Him up for the others to see.

"He's awake!" Micah exclaimed. "And He seems to be smiling at me!"

"He's awake because you're so loud," Nathaniel scolded.

"It's fine," Mary said. "Time for him to eat." She threw a cloak over her shoulder and then proceeded to nurse. "Joseph and I both noticed how the skies looked especially bright last night. Tell us more," she encouraged.

"The first angel that appeared said, 'I bring you good news of great joy that will be for all the people: Today in the city of David a Savior has been born to you. He is Christ the Lord!' Suddenly there were angels everywhere – too many to count. Multitudes of angels began praising God saying, 'Glory to God in the highest, and on earth peace to men on whom His favor rests!' I was sure the whole world could hear it, their voices boomed like thunder."

"Then what happened?" asked Joseph, leaning in on every word.

"Then, they disappeared..." said Joshua.

"...and we decided," Nathaniel cut in, "why don't we go to Bethlehem and see this thing for ourselves?"

"And we found you right away!" said Micah. "Just like the angel said!"

"Have you told anyone else about your experience – besides us?" Mary wanted to know.

"Of course. We told everyone we saw. They were amazed to know a Savior's been born! 'Peace on earth to ALL men,' the angel said! Why wouldn't we share the greatest news of all time?"

Mary gave Joseph a wary look and pondered all these things in her heart. *Maybe her Son wasn't born to be a King or a ruler. Could it be that He was born to be a sacrifice? Now what, Lord?*

Luke 2:6-20
http://biblicalleadership.com
http://chabad.org

XXI

BRIT MILAH & BRIT BAT – THE RITUALS

After the shepherds left, Mary and Joseph were left in deep thought over what the men had said. Mary kept many of her thoughts private. She promised God she would protect her newborn with everything she had.

"Today, you rest and take care of the Baby," Joseph said. "I'm going to look for a place where we can stay awhile. At least until your time of purification is over."

"We're going to stay here for forty days?" Mary asked. "I thought you'd want to get back home to Nazareth and to your business."

"I can find odd jobs here. It's more important to have you and the Baby healthy and strong before we get on the road again."

"We still need to register for the census," Mary said.

"We have a week before the deadline. A couple of more days, and you'll be up and about. For now, rest. I'll be back shortly. Pray I find something."

Mary knew better than to argue. She bade him goodbye and then laid down for a nap while her Son was sleeping. He would be soon awake, wanting to be fed. Before dozing off, she sighed. *I should have told Joseph to send word to Elizabeth.*

Joseph returned with exuberance a few hours later. "Mary! I found a place. It's not much, but it's sturdy – built into the hillside rock. I bumped into a distant cousin in town. He knew of this small house that will suit us just fine."

Admiration was evident in her voice. "May God be praised. Thank you, Joseph, for being so diligent in taking care of us." Her voice turned somber. "But didn't that take much of our savings?"

"Not for you to worry about, my dove. My cousin also knows of people needing work. We can move in as soon as you're able."

"Great," said Mary, knowing in her heart and by his look they were probably in debt. "Can we get word to Elizabeth and Zechariah in Jerusalem? She will want to see the Baby."

"Already done, my love," he replied.

#

It was almost a week since the Baby's birth, and the couple was now settled into their new home.

"Tomorrow makes the eighth day since the Baby was born," said Joseph. "Time for his circumcision and naming ceremony. Not only is it our Jewish tradition, it is also our devout duty according to God's law."

"Yes, and Elizabeth and Zechariah are coming for His Brit Milah and Brit Bat! I'm excited to see them again. They'll be here bright and early. Cousin Zechariah seemed very honored to be asked to perform the ritual ceremony. As a priest in the synagogue, he is skilled as a mohel."

"I would much rather he perform it than I," Joseph gave an involuntary shudder. "Circumcision is a covenant sign marking the first-born son as belonging to God, even though this Child already belongs to God."

As soon as the sun rose the next day, Joseph and Mary prepared the Babe and took Him to the Bethlehem synagogue. Elizabeth, Zechariah, and baby John would meet them there. Mary was overjoyed to see her parents waiting at the temple upon arrival.

"How did you know?" Mary hurried to hug her mother.

"I knew when you left that you didn't have long before delivery, daughter." Her mother laughed. "All of Nazareth is abuzz about the birth of your son. Many say he's Joseph's child and that he came a little too quickly." She chuckled as she lifted the blanket to see the Babe's face. "Aw…He's beautiful, Mary. But we know better. We couldn't wait to see him, so we counted the days and knew today would be his Bris."

Zechariah, the priest, took the Christ Child into his arms and said a blessing. Then he performed the ritual of Brit Milah and removed the boy's foreskin.

"Mazel tov!" cheered the witnesses.

"According to custom, today marks the beginning of this boy's life," exclaimed Mary's father.

"Now for the Brit Bat – the naming ceremony," said the priest. "What shall this child be called?"

Mary knew the name the angel gave her for her Son, but it was customary for the father to name the child. "Should we name him after you, Joseph?"

"No, Mary. I cannot have that honor. His name shall be called Jesus – just as the angel told me. Jesus Emmanuel, which means, 'He will save his people, for now God is truly with us.'"

Mary glowed with knowing. "We will name Him Jesus, as the angel proclaimed to us both."

"Scriptures also say He shall be called wonderful counselor, prince of peace, everlasting father," added Elizabeth.

"Ah, yes. He is destined for royalty," Mary's father said with pride in his voice. "And his mother with him."

Mary bit her lip and wanted to change this conversation quickly. "I have fresh fig cakes and grapes back at the house. Come celebrate with us."

"When will you come back home?" Mary's mother asked as they walked to the house. "I want this little one closer."

"We are going to stay here until after my purification ritual and Jesus's dedication in Jerusalem."

"That's more than a month away." Her eyes revealed sadness.

"It's the best way, Mother. Joseph has work here, and we have family close by. God will take care of us. He always has."

#

"Isn't it strange?" Mary pondered as they retired for the evening. "The blameless Son of God has subjected Himself to follow the way of Jehovah with the first drops of His pure and holy blood. It truly shows us how important it is to be in covenant relationship with Father God and to keep His commands."

Matthew 1:21-23

Luke 2:21

Isaiah 9:6

http://chicagojewishnews.com/what-is-a-jewish-ritual-circumcision

http://chabad.org

XXII

DEDICATION REVELATION

I wish I had a lamb to offer for the burnt offering," Mary mused. "It would be a real thank offering to God for a safe and successful pregnancy and delivery."

Joseph nodded. "I know," he said as he put the two turtledoves in a homemade cage. "Selling the burro only brought in enough money to buy the birds and have the five shekels needed to redeem Jesus from temple duty. Levitical law says we can substitute the birds for the lamb. Are you almost ready?"

Mary packed a clean change of clothes and checked on Jesus one more time. "I am. I can't wait to immerse myself in the mikveh and feel clean again. These forty days seemed to stretch on forever."

Reaching Jerusalem after the six-mile walk, the little family entered the city through the southern gate of the walled city.

"Here we are. The Lion's Gate," Mary commented. Perhaps Jesus will become like a lion – a strong and fierce ruler – the king of all Jews from the tribe of Judah!"

"The Lion of Judah?" Joseph grinned at his young wife's ingenuity. "I like it."

They found the mikveh, the freshwater bath in Jerusalem, on the southern wall of the temple at the base of the Double Gate stairs. A recent rainfall ensured the waters were flowing clean, God-given, and pure.

The procedure was dictated by the Torah that any woman bearing a man-child must present herself for purification rites forty days after birth. The procedure made her ritually clean and free to resume intimate relations with her husband.

Mary stepped down into the pool and then immersed herself in its clean waters, glad to finally be rid of her impurities. The holy moment embedded within her soul the commitment she had made to Jehovah. *I promise to care for your Son, Father God. We will raise Him right.*

Joseph waited outside with the Baby. Mary joined them when she finished, and they entered the temple and found the treasury.

"The firstborn son belongs to the Lord," said the treasury keeper. "He will be required to work in the temple when he's older unless you pay the fee."

"We have the required five shekels," said Joseph, handing the man the coins. "And here are our two turtledoves as required by law for Mary's purification and the dedication of our son."

Farther into the temple, they were met by a resident from Jerusalem who happened to be at synagogue that day.

"We have come to dedicate our son to Jehovah," Joseph said.

The aged man looked upon the Baby in Mary's arms. She watched as the man's eyes softened with wonder and adoration."

"I am Simeon," he said. "The Lord compelled me to come to the temple today. Now I know why. May I hold the child?"

Taking Baby Jesus in his arms, tears brimmed in his eyes. "I have been praying for someone to save Israel. I've waited for years. I have been watching for the Messiah to come. Jehovah promised I would not die until I saw Him."

Stroking the Baby's hair, he looked lovingly at the child's face. "Today, I have seen Israel's anointed king. Now I can die in content. I have seen the Messiah, just as God promised. I am holding the Savior you brought into the world. He is the Light that will shine upon the nations, and he will be the glory of your people, Israel."

Mary and Joseph stood in awe at his words. They gave each other questioning looks.

Simeon prayed a blessing upon the child. Then placing Jesus back in his mother's arms, he said to her, "A sword shall pierce your soul, for this child shall be rejected by many in Israel; this is to their undoing. But He will be the greatest joy among many others, and the deep thoughts of many will be revealed."

While Simeon spoke, an elderly lady passing by stopped to listen. Seeing Jesus, her face lit up with joy. She began to bless the child with praises and worship, telling all those nearby, "Here is Jerusalem's redemption child!"

"This is Anna, the prophetess," Simeon explained, "who worships God night and day. After her husband died only seven years into her marriage, she came here to live."

"I am now 84 years old," Anna nodded. "I've prayed and fasted for years for Israel. Today I have seen God's gift to mankind. Thank you, Yahweh." She raised her head in worship again. "Thank you for showing me your Savior – the hope of the whole world."

Looking Mary in the eye, she said, "I've been telling everyone in Jerusalem. The Messiah has come! I've been waiting for many, many years, but now I know for sure – He's here!!"

Mary and Joseph left Jerusalem that day in confusion, wonder, curiosity, and joy.

"I have no more doubts, Mary," Joseph confessed. "This Baby – your Son – is God's Son indeed. There have been way too many confirmations to think anything else."

Mary was quiet the rest of the way home, troubled by many thoughts. She was ecstatic with joy but also worried in her spirit. *The prophetess was telling everyone in Jerusalem that the Messiah has been born. The shepherds were spreading the news that Jesus was to be the Savior of the world. Nazareth already knew about the birth. How far would this news go? Was Jesus in danger? ...and what did Simeon mean that a sword would pierce my soul?*

Luke 2:22-38 (The Way); Leviticus 12:1-8

http://Livescience.com/49997

http://Earlychurchhistory.org

http://Missionspaul.com/2018/12/30

http://Jerusalemperspective.com/4004

http://Encyclopedia.com/religion

https://www.generationword.com=jerusalem101 › 39-mikvah-ritual-baths.html

https://theheartofisrael.org › the-mikvah-the-jewish-ritual-bath-house

https://jwa.org/encyclopedia/article/mikveh

XXIII

A STAR, A KING, & A ROYAL VISIT

On a clear, bright night in southern Arabia, three astrologers searched the skies. As counselors to the King of Sheba, their sole occupation was to interpret the stars and forecast the future.

"Gasper!" Melchior sounded excited. "Come look at this!"

Gasper joined Melchior and Balthazar on the upper floor to view the starry expanse.

"Look at the brightness of that star. Like one we've never seen before," Balthazar said. "It's like the Northern Star, but so much larger!"

"It's a sign," agreed Gasper. "We must research the scrolls."

As scientists, they witnessed an unexplainable phenomenon. As philosophers, they recognized the noteworthy event. But they also believed it to be a sign of a coming Jewish king.

Balthazar called out. "I found it! It's in part of Moses' Pentateuch, the scroll of Numbers. "A star shall come out of Jacob; a scepter shall rise out of Israel."

"We must inform the King immediately," said Melchior.

Receiving an audience before the King of Sheba, they bowed. Then Gasper said, "O honorable King, it is our duty to inform you of world-wide events as we consult the stars. The prophet Isaias said, 'the nations come in adoration and praise of a king and bring gold and frankincense in his honor.'"*

After they finished telling him what they'd seen, he replied, "You must go find this new king of the Jews and honor him. Take gold from my treasury which houses much of the vast gold from the Sheba mines. Also, take some aromatic frankincense and myrrh that is abundant here."

The men headed toward Israel within the week.

"Jerusalem is a good place to start, don't you think?" asked Melchior.

"The capital city? Yes! What better place to search for a king?" replied Gasper.

They arrived many months later following the mysterious star over hot desert sand from Sheba traveling northwest through Arabia. Entering Jerusalem's busy marketplace, they began asking vendors, "Where is he who's been born the King of the Jews? We have come to worship Him. Tell us where he might be found?"

Their royal-looking presence and questions sent the city in a stir, wondering who these noble and highly-educated men were.

One vendor grew excited. "It's true. A baby was born not far from here a little over two years ago. Everyone was talking about it then. They said the angels made a proclamation to some shepherds, calling this child the King of the Jews, the Savior of the world."

"They said the angel told them the child was destined to be a king who will bring peace and goodwill toward men. Many people doubted, but many others were glad."

"We need a change in this government," said another. "A new king who will take down this Roman tyranny."

The three travelers gave their acknowledgment. "Where was the child born?" they asked. "We have gifts for him."

"Bethlehem – about six miles southwest in the hills. It's a very small village. If King Herod knew about his birth, he'd be furious. He's been known to kill his own family for the sake of protecting his throne."

The other vendor's laugh was guarded as he whispered. "Caesar Augustus once said that it was safer to be Herod's pig than his son. Use caution in dealing with this king."

"It's rumored that some people are even forming a rogue coalition to bring Herod down," another whispered. "But don't repeat that to anyone!" The man looked around for hearing ears.

Nearby, a servant from the palace kitchen overheard the conversation. She ran back to the palace and told the other servants. The news spread like wildfire. It didn't take long for the king to hear, and it was news to him.

#

Intense fear struck King Herod's heart when he learned of a Jewish king being born. Herod was not of Jewish heritage, yet he had been installed as king of Judah. If a royal heir had been born, his kingship was in jeopardy. With hysteria dilating his wild eyes, Herod summoned his scribes and high priests.

"Why didn't you tell me?" he screamed in manic rage. "You are supposed to know these things! How am I to rule without proper knowledge?"

Seeing his rage, they cowered in silence.

His glare threatened. "You know that a royal heir to King David's throne presents a threat to me."

"Your Majesty," one of the priests attempted to calm him. "A child is hardly a threat."

The king wiped the sweat from his brow as he paced the marble floor. His face turned crimson. "I want this child found. Tell me where this 'king' lives. NOW!"

As the priests scurried from the room like frightened mice, King Herod held one back. "Go bring these men to me. I want a private meeting with them. From what I hear, they won't be too hard to find."

By the end of the day, the three Wisemen found themselves standing before King Herod.

"Tell me, noblemen, how did you learn of this new 'king'?"

"We saw his star in the sky. It led us here. We've come to pay homage to him."

Herod's eyes narrowed and his teeth gritted in anger, but he contained his wrath. Fuming in his heart but feigning interest, he controlled his words. "When exactly did you see this star appear?"

When they told him all they knew, the king related the prophet Micah's words. "The priests told me a leader would come from Bethlehem. So, go now. Find this king, and then come back and tell me where he is so I may go worship him too." Herod's words gushed with mock sincerity.

The astrologers agreed, not knowing King Herod had much more nefarious ideas in his paranoid mind.

Matthew 2:1-8 (The Way); Numbers 24:17-(NKJV) Isaiah 60:6;
Micah 5:2; Daniel 9:25-26; Exodus 30:34
https://sermonwriter.com/biblical-commentary/new-testament-matthew-21-12/
http://crosswalk.com/specialcoverage/christmas-and-advent
http://bibleinfo.com
http://whychristmas.com/story/wisemen
http://Missionspaul.com/2018/12/30
http://Jerusalemperspective.com/4004

XXIV

GIFTS FOR A KING

The three set off the next day on the hour-or-so walk to Bethlehem, anxious to find the new king. Their journey had been long.

Balthazar spoke as they walked. "King Herod sounded sincere when he talked to us, but his countenance spoke of jealousy."

Gasper nodded. "He said he wanted us to search carefully and find the child so he could go worship him, too. But can we trust him?"

Melchior spoke. "A man in the marketplace told me King Herod guards his throne with ferocity. Said he's even killed several wives and his father-in-law to ensure his reign over Judah."

Balthazar gasped. "He is that suspicious about someone taking his throne?"

"He also warned us to be cautious in our dealings with King Herod. We would be wise to heed his words," continued Melchior.

Entering Bethlehem, Gasper noted, "We need to search for the child. Should we start in the marketplace again, or go door to door?"

No sooner did Gasper finish speaking than Balthazar exclaimed with awe, "Well! Would you look at that?!" He pointed upward. "Our star is back! And it seems to be guiding us toward the hills on the edge of town."

"Impossible!" Melchior raised his head to view the anomaly. "Stars do not travel!"

"This one does!" laughed Gasper. "This is amazing! He must truly be a special king."

And so, they followed the star until it rested over a small house built into the rocky hillside. A toddler was playing outside while his mother tended her small garden.

Seeing the royal noblemen approach, Mary quickly went to her son and picked Him up. Her concern was evident.

"It is He!" said Gasper. "The One we've searched for!"

All three bowed before Mary and Jesus. "Your Majesty," they said in unison.

"Please forgive us for intruding, my lady, but we've traveled for many days from a distant land to worship this new king of the Jews," said Melchior.

"We followed His star," Balthazar pointed upward, "after searching the scrolls for its meaning and truth. Now, look! See how it shines about His holiness? Even the heavens are pleased to honor this King."

Mary was dumbfounded at their pronouncement and left speech-less. Gathering her composure, she acknowledged them with a nod.

"Oh, where are my manners?" She apologized. "Please come into my humble abode. My name is Mary, and this is my Son, Jesus."

The men smiled at the befuddled young mother and followed her inside.

Setting Jesus down, she asked, "May I offer you some water or fruit?"

"No, we cannot stay. We must return to our homes and spread this good news. But first," said Melchior, "we brought gifts for the King." He kneeled before Mary and the toddler and set a golden chest on the floor. "I bring pure gold from the vast storehouses of Sheba. This signifies that we acknowledge Jesus as the true King of the Jews."

Gasper gave Mary an alabaster jar and then kneeled before Jesus. "To King Jesus, I offer the fine aromatic frankincense resin from Sheba's Boswellian tree."

Balthazar came and kneeled with the others and handed Mary a beautiful, ornate flask. "Within this flask is fragrant myrrh from the Commiphora tree. Its anointing oil celebrates the King for His glory and honor. With these gifts, we offer our worship and adoration to our God who has led us here."

"Jesus will be a wise and righteous king and a scepter in Israel," said Gasper.

The noblemen left the house full of joy. They would stay at the Bethlehem Inn for the night and then head back to Jerusalem the following day, as planned.

As they left, Mary could hardly contain her joy. Joseph would be home soon, and she couldn't wait to tell him.

#

The following day the men began their journey back toward the capital city. Gasper suddenly stopped mid-stride. "I know we promised King Herod that we would return and tell him where Jesus could be found, but I feel a foreboding in my spirit."

Balthazar agreed. "I know what you mean. I'm not sure King Herod has pure motives in seeking this king. Perhaps we shouldn't reveal where the child lives."

"I had a strange dream last night," Melchior began. "I wasn't going to say anything, but...."

"But what, Melchoir? Speak up."

"I dreamt King Herod was seeking Jesus for evil reasons – too abhorrent to mention. In my dream, he was brutal and wicked. I believe we need to find another way home and not pass through Jerusalem."

The other two nodded in agreement. So, the three left the Judean hills to return to Arabia another way without seeing King Herod.

Melchior could not imagine how close his dream was to the truth.

Numbers 24:17: Matthew 2:7-14
http://www.bibleinfo.com
http://www.whychristmas.com

XXV

PARANOIA

King Herod became suspicious when one day turned into three without hearing from the Wisemen.

"Did they not understand that I wanted to hear from them? Or, did they just not find that boy? Why haven't they come back?" Herod paced the floor as he questioned his advisors. "Or – did they trick me?"

The king's advisors attempted to calm and dissuade his fears. His explosive temper was common knowledge, and they did not want to stir his wrath. He could become quite volatile when angered. Being sick and angry was double jeopardy.

"Please sit," one said, "you're shaking. Rabbi Alexander, call for the king's doctor."

"I DON'T NEED a doctor," Herod coughed. Putrid sputum flew and the advisors danced as the rabbi hurried out the door.

Herod continued to rant. "Why didn't Caesar Augustus tell me where this boy was born in the first place?" he snapped. "Surely, he must have known. The family registered in his census! He would have known where they lived. Wouldn't Augustus want to keep me on the throne where he and the Roman Senate placed me?"

Swaying his head from side to side, Herod's voice rose with each word. "I TOLD them to come back. I TOLD them to tell me where this child could be found. WHERE ARE THEY?" His arms flailed the air as he seethed.

The king's doctor quickly came and assessed the situation. "Everyone, leave. Please. His Majesty needs rest. Sir, you will bring on convulsions again in this state," he said sternly. "Calm yourself."

The doctor administered salve to the king's sores noting that the disease was getting worse. "Lay down and rest," he commanded, waiting until the king obeyed.

Reluctantly, Herod lay down, but with incensed thoughts and plans on how to find this 'king of the Jews.'

#

With each passing day, he became more livid. By the end of the week, King Herod was convinced he had been outwitted by the magi, and he was outraged.

"That boy will NOT take my throne!" He cursed the filthy air he breathed. "No one -- and I mean NO one will take my place! Especially some lowly child born in a barn. What kind of royalty is that?"

A servant, hearing his loud tirade, ran into his quarters. "Your Majesty." Stumbling back at the stench in the room, the boy quickly bowed but did not turn his back on an outraged king with murder in his eyes. "Can I help you?"

"GET OUT!" the king screamed through breath foul enough to kill an ox.

The servant turned to run but the king shouted after him, "WAIT!" Maintaining control for a slight moment, he spoke more softly. "Send in my advisors." When the boy didn't leave immediately, his anger returned. "NOW!"

As the king's counselors entered, they blocked their noses with their sleeves. The king's condition was getting worse. They frowned with knowing and gave each other a nonverbal warning to stay quiet as they witnessed the crazed king.

"What should I do? I've already disposed of anyone threatening my throne...."

"Including your wife's whole family," someone muttered under his breath.

The others gave him a somber warning glance.

"They were conspiring against me!" Herod's eyes narrowed and his face flushed with anger as he wheezed. "And I'll kill every one of them if they dare to...."

"Oh, great King," another advisor cut him short, "Why not send a convoy into Bethlehem?" Keeping his voice soft and soothing, he continued. "Go door to door. Search for the child. Then, when you find him, you can decide whether to banish the family or imprison them."

"Yes," agreed another. "This will give you time to make a wise decision."

King Herod stopped pacing and absentmindedly scratched at an ulcerous sore. "When did the magi first say the star appeared?"

His advisors quickly consulted with one another and then answered. "It was over two years ago, Your Highness."

Herod stroked his beard while chewing the inside of his lip. "Hmmm...ye-e-s-s." He drew out the word. But another much more demonic thought tickled his evil mind.

Matthew 2:16-18; Jeremiah 31:15
http://Learningreligions.com
http://bibleodyssey.com

XXVI

MURDER OF INNOCENCE

By week two, King Herod was ready to tear out his hair and scratch his skin raw. The magi had duped him – and someone would pay. He summoned his soldiers.

"Go at once to Bethlehem. Search for the boy they call the 'king of the Jews.'"

The captain of the guard nodded. "How will we know if we find the right boy?"

Herod gave him a frustrated glance. "It's been rumored the magi brought the family expensive gifts. Search each house in the village and in the surrounding vicinities. If you find any evidence of something that looks out of place for a poor peasant, you'll know you that was the boy's home."

"We will leave at once, Your Highness." He turned to leave, satisfied he had his command.

"Wait – I'm not finished speaking," the king yelled. "I haven't dismissed you yet."

The captain froze in place and turned around to face the king.

"Don't you ever leave my presence unless I give you permission, Captain. Understood?"

The man nodded and swallowed hard.

"When you get to Bethlehem, I want you to go door to door. Search every home, like I said. But here's more. If there are any boys aged two and under, seize them. Then KILL them," his voice rose in fury. "We will make sure to stamp out this idea of kingship in Israel. UNDERSTAND?"

The captain nodded once more as his insides turned to jelly.

"And don't return until the job is done. Don't forget to search all the areas surrounding Bethlehem, too."

The captain dared not question, or his head would roll. His soldiers would obey his orders, no matter how dark or evil they seemed. Consequences for failure or disobedience were swift and harsh.

#

People stared and wondered why a band of soldiers would come to town. This little town had nothing to offer. They didn't have to wonder long. It was about to become Bethlehem's darkest day.

In the marketplace, a woman hoisted her baby boy on her hip as she sniffed the aroma of fresh apples. The soldier approached from behind and ripped the baby from her arms.

"My baby!" she screamed as the child slipped from her grasp. She grabbed the baby's legs and held on tight, but not before the soldier viciously took his dagger and slit the baby's throat. Tossing the limp child back at her, her shriek was drowned out by other mothers experiencing the same horrific nightmare.

"Why? Why?" the mothers wailed in agony. But no words of explanation or sympathy were given.

Then, heading into the neighborhood, soldiers searched each house as the king commanded. They found nothing extraordinary in town but killed many little boys in their murderous path anyway.

No place was too sacred. The temple was ravaged as well. One brave father attacked a soldier who killed his son. Grappling the soldier to the ground only met the father with a dagger to his heart. Sorrowful priests and rabbis stood by in stark shock and dismay.

"Today scripture has been fulfilled," cried one rabbi. "As our Prophet Jeremiah said, 'There shall be weeping in Ramah....'"*

Making a full sweep of the village, the soldiers wiped their bloody blades. Next stop: the hill country on the outskirts of Bethlehem – where Mary and Joseph lived.

When no one answered the knock at Joseph and Mary's home, they broke down the door and searched the place. It was empty of clothes and food.

One of the soldiers picked up the empty flask and sniffed inside. "Myrrh. They were here. This was the child's house." In anger, he flung the flask against the wall, smashing it into bits.

"They're gone...and we've failed."

———————————————

Matthew 2:16-18; Jeremiah 31:15
http://Learningreligions.com
http://bibleodyssey.com

XXVII

FLIGHT IN THE NIGHT

The day before the soldiers arrived, Mary hummed a little tune as she prepared the evening meal. Deciding Bethlehem would be a good place to live and raise Jesus, they had settled in. God had provided for them and protected them. Joseph had secured many carpentry jobs and was able to sell his wares in Jerusalem. Mary was happy and her heart overflowed. *Thank you for your faithfulness, Father.*

Checking on Jesus, she found him contently playing with a wooden toy Joseph carved. He was growing into a strong and healthy little boy. She looked lovingly into his handsome face. *So, is this what You look like, God?* She wondered.

Jesus looked up at his mama and smiled. *You're handsome and kind, with soft eyes and a welcoming smile?* She gave her Son a squeeze. "I love you, Jesus."

During the meal, she and Joseph spoke of the Wisemen and the extravagant gifts they had received.

"We're so blessed, Joseph. But this also troubles my spirit. If news of Jesus's birth has traveled so far that even royalty came from the East to worship Him...." Mary's voice caught in her throat. Her forehead wrinkled in worry. "Joseph – is Jesus in danger?"

Joseph gave his young wife a look of adoration and admiration. So strong and yet so discerning for one so young. He didn't want her to fret, but he also knew King Herod's reputation. One minute a benevolent king who pleased the Jews with new buildings; the next minute, a brutal tyrant placating the Romans by charging heavy taxes and fierce mandates. Joseph knew Herod would stop at nothing if he perceived his throne to be threatened. His mouth tightened into a thin line as his own thoughts tied into a knot in his stomach.

"Joseph? What do you think? Should we be worried?"

"We'll be fine, my dear. God will take care of us." He squeezed Mary's shoulder. "Isn't that what you always say? God will protect His Son – and His Son's mother. And I will do my very best to do my part, too."

Mary gave Joseph a warm smile. "I know you will. You always know what to say to help me feel safe. Thank you, my love."

Joseph walked over to the shelf where the golden chest sat along with the alabaster jar and flask of myrrh. He pulled a rawhide pouch from his belt. "These gifts are beyond belief," commented Joseph as he began to put coins into the pouch.

"Their whole story was amazing," agreed Mary. "Did you know they traveled over one thousand miles to come here, and not just to see Jesus, but to honor him as royalty and worship His deity. They knew, Joseph."

"What are you doing?" she asked as she watched him empty the gold chest.

"I'm packing the gold coins into this easy-to-carry pouch for safer keeping. This gold must be worth many years of wages. We'll pack the frankincense resin too. Do you have a smaller bottle we can use for the myrrh?"

"These resins are worth much more value than the gold. The Wisemen have given us anointing oil, antiseptic, medicine, perfume, and more in these two spices. Priests use frankincense as a sacrifice when it's burned at the synagogue. It is the only pure and holy incense allowed."

"Well, perhaps we could sell some for Jesus's education later on?" Mary mused.

"That's a conversation for another day." Joseph laughed. "For now, it will help provide in the days ahead."

Mary tucked Jesus in bed for the night. As Joseph drifted off to sleep, his mind tumbled with thoughts of the magi, King Herod's paranoia, and the great wealth they had just acquired. Restless, he tossed and turned until another dream emerged.

An angel appeared to him saying loud and clear, "Joseph! Get up. Take Mary and the Child and flee to Egypt. Tonight. Do not wait. Stay there until you hear word that it's okay to return. Hurry."

Joseph bolted upright in bed in a cold sweat. The dream seemed so real. Shaking visibly, he awakened Mary. "Mary. Get up. Dress quickly."

"What's wrong?" Mary rubbed the sleep from her eyes. Seeing Jesus was still asleep, she rolled over to look at Joseph.

"The angel warned me to take you and Jesus to Egypt."

She yawned. "Can't it wait until morning?" She rolled back over and pulled the covers over her.

"No, Mary. The angel's message was urgent. We must leave. To-night. Gather all the food we can carry. Prepare a couple of flasks of water and pack all your clothes. We won't be coming back. Hurry."

Her voice held sudden alarm. "Are we....is Jesus...in peril, Joseph?"

"Yes, He is. King Herod seeks to hurt Jesus. The angel was adamant that we leave right away tonight."

#

As they hurriedly packed, Joseph grabbed the pouch of gold coins and stuffed them into his satchel along with the flasks of water. He was glad God gave him the forethought to pack it for easy carrying.

"What about the chest and flask?" Mary asked.

"We'll leave them here. It will pay for our house. Ready to go?"

Mary made a sling of fabric to wrap around her so Jesus could ride on her back, and Joseph slung the satchel over his back.

And so it was that in the middle of the night, the little family headed southwest toward the land of Egypt and fulfilled the scripture, "I will call my Son out of Egypt."

Matthew 2:13-15; Hosea 11:1
http://History.com;
http://tctimes.com/gifts-of-the-wisemen/

XXVIII

JOURNEY INTO EGYPT

Unaware of the atrocious slaughter of all the innocent little boys in and around Bethlehem, Joseph, Mary, and Jesus turned west toward Gaza by the Mediterranean Sea.

"We'll continue to follow the seashore," Joseph said. "It will take us all the way to Alexandria. I have heard there are many thriving Jewish communities there."

The trio stopped in a shaded grassy area to have a breakfast of fig cakes and rest awhile. Mary kept a watchful eye on Jesus as he wandered offroad toward some bushes.

"Such an inquisitive boy," Joseph commented.

"He loves to explore, even at this age. A typical two-year-old, I suppose," said Mary.

No sooner had she turned her back than Jesus began to cry. Mary hurried to Him to see what was wrong. With tears in His eyes, He held up His finger. She knelt beside Him and took His hand in hers, examining it carefully.

"You must watch out for the thornbushes, Son," she said with a stern note. She pulled the thorn from Jesus's finger and then reached in her satchel for the bottle of myrrh. Soaking a tiny corner of her veil in the oil, she dabbed Jesus's finger. "There you go, sweet boy," she cooed softly in his ear. She wiped away his tears with another corner of her garment and then kissed His cheek.

Jesus tightly hugged her neck. "Love you, Mama." Then off he scampered off to explore the world.

"That boy!" exclaimed Mary. "He did find us some luscious berries, though." As she leaned back against a tree and popped a couple of blackberries into her mouth, she pondered. "What do you think God has planned for Him?"

"The prophet called Him the Prince of peace. Maybe He'll be crowned prince before He becomes the King of the Jews," thought Joseph.

"Prophet Isaiah also called Him 'wonderful counselor'. Perhaps people will come from all over the world to receive counsel from Him," dreamed Mary.

"Well," Joseph said, "the angel told me He would save people from their sins. That's why we named Him Jesus."

"As he also told me," recalled Mary. "The Savior and Messiah. That's so hard to fathom right now." She watched Jesus crouch to examine the ants crawling on the ground. "He seems like just a normal little boy who loves to play."

"We know He's destined for great things. It's still too incredible. All I know is that I promised to raise Him in the fear and admonition of the Lord. And I will do that to the best of my ability. We just have to be ready. For the time being, let's rest while we're out of harm's way. Then, we'll head farther out of King Herod's jurisdiction. It's going to be a long journey."

It turned out to be longer than they thought with having a little boy still in diapers. By the end of two weeks, they finally reached the city of Alexandria. As they neared the big city, Mary prayed.

Help us, Father God, to find favor. We trust you for continued protection and help.

The marketplace was always a good source of information. "There's a large Jewish community in the eastern sector by the seashore," they were informed. Seeing all the artisans and Jewish merchants, Joseph felt assured in his spirit he'd made the right decision coming this far.

They spent the next two years in Alexandria, finding new life in Egypt. Their wealth afforded them good stature in the community and a nice home. They discovered a wonderful Jewish community where they met new friends. Joseph earned reputable recognition in the field of construction.

Mary's soul overflowed. God had fulfilled His promise to be ever watchful and protect and provide for every detail. She knew she could trust Father God for Jesus's future and for theirs as well.

But many other thoughts clouded her mind, too. And those she stashed away – some to be treasured – some to be pondered.

Later.

Matthew 2:14, 15

https://christ.org/history-rituals/where-did-mary-and-joseph-take-jesus-in-egypt/

https://www.biblestudytools.com/classics/andrews-the-life-of-our-lord-upon-the-earth/part-i/jesus-in-egypt.html

https://www.jewishvirtuallibrary.org/alexandria

https://aleteia.org/2017/12/29/where-did-the-holy-family-live-in-egypt/

XXIX

CONSEQUENCES

Meanwhile, back in Jerusalem –

The captain of the guard dreaded the report he was obligated to give King Herod. Even though many children were mercilessly slaughtered, the soldiers had failed to find King Jesus.

"Tell me you found him," King Herod demanded. "Tell me I no longer have to worry about losing my kingdom."

"Your kingship is safe, Your Majesty," assured the captain.

"You found him, then? You killed him?"

"You have nothing to worry about, sir."

King Herod wasn't about to be duped again. He glared at the captain. "What aren't you telling me?" he yelled.

"We found the house where the child lived, Majesty. But it was empty. They were gone."

"And...? Tell me you searched all over town and country to find them."

"Uh...." The soldier hesitated. "We had already searched all of the houses."

"And you didn't search again?" the king screeched.

"No, sir." The captain hung his head for the last time, knowing his fate was sealed.

"YOU and your men," Herod's voice raised, "will find your own destiny with the sword. Say goodbye, Captain." He sneered while motioning the guards in the room. "Seize him and his men. Tomorrow, they die."

Consequences were extreme for those who violated the king's law – but even higher for those who defied God's law.

#

The few months following the heinous event took King Herod down a dark path. His fury knew no bounds. It devoured his soul. The last despicable deed of killing children ate him alive. One priest called it God's judgment upon the king.

He was often short of breath with chest pains and debilitating pain in his abdomen. His disposition became as foul as the stench of his body.

Family affairs weren't any better. He was suspicious of everyone, including his ten wives and fourteen children. Herod's eldest son, Antipater, fed into his paranoia.

"I'm the rightful heir to your throne," Antipater told his father. "But your other wife, Mariamne, and her two sons are conspiring against you. They are plotting to assassinate you to take your throne."

Convincing Herod of the worst, Antipater succeeded in his devious plot, and Mariamne and her two sons were executed.

Besides the pain in his belly, the itching of his lower parts drove him insane. When it became too excruciating to bear, he called for his doctor, the only one who could speak freely without fear of retaliation. The doctor examined Herod and was appalled at the decomposition he witnessed.

"You stink like a walking corpse," the doctor was blunt. "Your body is literally eating itself from the inside out."

King Herod screamed in delirium as the doctor scraped the worms from the king's lower parts. "Mariamne! Send for my beloved at once," he cried out. "I need my sweet Mariamne!"

"Queen Mariamne is dead, Your Majesty. Remember? You had her killed – along with her mother, her brother, and her two sons."

The king's eyes went wild with realization. "She was trying to poison me! Antipater said so."

"I know you love your first-born, Majesty. You lavishly granted him a high place in the government. But Antipater is not as loyal as you think. He is a deceiver and manipulator. He conspired against Mariamne and her sons to gain the throne for himself."

Herod began to shake uncontrollably. "No. NO! It can't be true. Antipater looks out for me."

"Think what you want, Sire, but an investigation would be in order."

Soon after the doctor left, King Herod demanded his counselors investigate the charges against his son, Antipater. They soon returned with damaging news.

"It is true, Majesty. Reports say that your first-born son, Antipater, was the one conspiring against you all along. He spread rumors about his stepbrothers until you had them executed. Now he's attacking his other stepbrothers. He said, 'if the king's life keeps dragging on, I will never get the throne.' Antipater is a dangerous man."

Herod's face flushed as his eye popped in rage. "Send in my lawyers. Consider my son disinherited! I'm changing my will! Throw Antipater into the palace prison. Let him think about what he's done. He will not insult and humiliate me this way!"

As the men scrambled to obey, Herod ranted on. "And find five of the most prominent families in Jerusalem. Imprison them too..." He scratched at an incessant sore, "...and when I die, kill them all. I want it said that there was weeping in Jerusalem on the day I pass."

His counselors knew better than to question his insane thoughts. The orders to have the families imprisoned were carried out the next day.

Herod's necrotizing disease got progressively worse until it affected his mental capacities. With his favorite wife and sons gone, he had no hope. The rest of his family despised him; his subjects hated him. He wanted to die. It was only destiny that brought another son his way that day.

At the moment Herod raised the knife to plunge into his belly, Archelaus happened by the king's chamber. As the horror quickly registered in his mind, he rushed over to grab the blade from his father's grasp before it met its mark.

"Noooo!" Herod's loud groan sounded like a wounded animal.

Hearing his father's cry from his prison cell below, a smile broadened Antipater's face. "Guard! Many riches from the Herod's treasury will be yours if you release me. My father is dead. I must be crowned immediately."

The guard ran to see what had happened. When he saw King Herod had survived his suicide attempt, he reported to the king what his son, Antipater said.

In anguished outrage, King Herod sent word to execute Antipater immediately along with the five families that were imprisoned."

The palace guards dutifully carried out the king's command, killing Antipater but not the families, recognizing the king's insanity.

Five days later, King Herod died. The families were released and instead of Jerusalem weeping, they rejoiced.

Herod's oldest surviving son, Archelaus, took the throne, and for a few days, Jerusalem took a fresh breath of relief.

King Herod was finally dead.

---

http://Brittanica.org

http://jewishencyclopedia.com

http://bibleprobe.com

http://newswise.com/articles/what-killed-king-herod

Book of Jewish Antiquities, Josephus

XXX

═══════

THE BEGINNING

Mary loved life in Egypt, although she missed her mother from time to time. Her mom was missing all of Jesus's firsts – his first steps, his first words, his first ideas. Her little boy was growing up way too fast. Now, at age four, he had a vast vocabulary and an amazing understanding of His world.

Mary's new friends were a source of joy as they gathered weekly at the temple. Joseph had steady work. They had settled in for the long haul. They would obey and stay there until they received a sign. Joseph didn't know how or when that would happen, but he remained vigilant. God had been faithful in giving direction.

Then one night, Joseph had another dream. It was the same angel who had given him previous direction and precaution. "Take the Child and His mother back to Israel," he said. "Those seeking to kill Him are dead."

The following morning, Joseph told Mary. "The angel appeared to me again last night. We can go home; it's safe to return."

"When?" she asked.

"As soon as we can, I guess. We'll have to sell our home, and I have a project to finish. But Passover is in a couple of months. Perhaps we can make it back to Jerusalem by then to celebrate. What do you think?"

"That sounds wonderful," said Mary, "I would love to celebrate Passover with Cousin Elizabeth again. Jesus can travel better now, so we could make it in two or three weeks. YES! Let's do it."

The couple started packing that very day, and Mary became more excited when their house sold so quickly.

"Joseph, where shall we live? Jerusalem would be a good place, don't you think? The capital city has rabbis where Jesus can go to school, and you could get a great job there."

"I think Bethlehem would be a better choice. The City of David, the city of Jesus's ancestors, is smaller and friendlier. Plus, we still have many friends there."

"And Jesus would have many playmates," Mary thought about other mothers with children Jesus's age. "And only a few minutes walk to Jerusalem."

Soon, the family was back on the road, this time headed straight east toward Giza by the Nile River, then north across the Sinai desert toward Judea.

"Look, Mama!" Jesus pointed to the large structure on the plains outside Giza. As they stopped to camp overnight, Jesus couldn't stop asking questions about the great pyramids.

As they neared Judea, they noticed many sojourners traveling away from Jerusalem. Fear registered on every face they passed. Joseph stopped one family to question them.

"Where's everyone going?" asked Joseph. "Aren't you going to Jerusalem for the Passover celebration?"

"Haven't you heard?" The man spoke in whispered tones and surveyed the area for listening ears. "King Herod died not long after he murdered all the children two and under in Bethlehem."

A shiver crawled up Mary's back as she gasped at the news. *We escaped just in time. Praise you, Yahweh.*

The man continued, "His son, Archelaus, took the throne. He's brutal and insane – just like his father, Herod."

Joseph's face turned white. Turning to Mary, he spoke in a low voice as he gave her a cautious look. "Why would the angel say it's safe if Herod's son is in control?" Turning back to the man, he asked, "Just like his father, you said?"

"Maybe worse," the traveler nodded in reply. "The new king has been entangled in a religious war, fighting insurrectionists. He canceled Passover and murdered over three thousand men and women in the temple."

"Oh, God. What do I do now?" Joseph prayed aloud. "Where do we go?"

Mary patted his arm. "God will work it out, Joseph. He always does. He will protect His Son."

As they lay down to sleep, the angel again appeared to Joseph and warned him not to go to Jerusalem or Bethlehem. Awakening refreshed, he knew just what to do. They would live outside the king's domain – in Galilee.

"Mary, what do you think about living farther north – in the land of Galilee again?"

Her eyes lit up, and she squealed with delight. "In Nazareth? By Jesus's grandparents? I love it! Now I'm really excited to go home, Joseph!"

"Then that's where we'll raise God's Son. I think I might still have a home around there somewhere."

And so, 'the Child grew and became strong. He was filled with wisdom, and the grace of God was upon Him.'

~~The End.~~

The Beginning.

Matthew 2:19-23; Hosea 11:1; Luke 2:39-40

http://Evidenceunseen.com/theology; http://bibleprobe.com

http://history.com; http://Brittanica.org; http://jewishencyclopedia.com

Book of Jewish Antiquities, Josephus

Thank you for reading *the chosen one*.

A review would be most welcomed!

C.A. Simonson is an award-winning writer and author from the beautiful Ozarks of Missouri. Her other Christian inspirational novels include the *Journey Home* trilogy: *Love's Journey Home, Love Looks Back,* and *Love's Amazing Grace,* and *RUNAWAY.* She has also written several nonfiction books and two children's activity books.

After retirement from a career in computer training/teaching, Candy turned her attention to writing and assisting other authors in seeing their dream of publication come true.

See more from C.A. Simonson at
http://casimonson.com